DYING BREATH

ERIK CARTER

ISBN: 9798311170086

CHAPTER ONE

Plymouth, Wisconsin
The 1990s

PEOPLE DIE FOR STRANGE REASONS.

Layne Grosicki understood that as well as anyone else.

His good college friend, Cam O'Hara, had survived bar fights, sports injuries, and even a daredevil-stunt-induced motorcycle crash—only to choke to death on an undercooked broccoli floret in the dining hall.

Then there was Uncle Stan. A trucker his whole life, Layne's uncle could handle any road, any weather, any time. But one summer afternoon—on a clear, empty highway—he toppled his rig after swerving to avoid a plastic lawn chair that had tumbled out of a pickup bed. No skid marks, no sign of trouble—just the engine idling, and Uncle Stan, gone.

Now Layne was to die like his friend and uncle had—because of something benign, trivial. In Layne's case, death wasn't coming by way of a vegetable or a piece of cheap lawn furniture...

...but cheese.

Cheese.

Specifically, discrepancies in shipping manifests tied to bulk shipments of artisanal cheese.

Discrepancies in shipping manifests. That phrasing made it sound important—like Layne had uncovered something sinister, like he was on the verge of exposing a hidden threat and would die for it. All of that was true. And it made his impending death feel noble, maybe even heroic.

But Layne's mind kept stripping the notion down, reducing it to its simplest form.

He was going to die for cheese.

Yes, die. No question about it. No way out. He was outnumbered and outmatched. And the guys hunting him were clearly elite tacticians. Layne was anything but.

No one had ever called Layne a quitter. But he was a realist.

Layne moved slowly. His boots scuffed against concrete. The late-night air was cool, tasted like rot. The abandoned facility stretched wide before him. Rows of rusted machinery faded into the darkness. Too many shadows. Too many places to hide. Moonlight slashed through broken windows, cutting the gloom into sharp angles. Somewhere out there, water dripped. Steady.

He paused. Listened.

Nothing.

Just that hollow, steady drip of water.

He moved on. Low and quiet. Weaving between hulking vats and twisted conveyor belts. He stopped to crouch behind a massive steel tank, pausing again.

He angled his face to the quiet beyond, listened even more intently. Now, he detected another gentle sound mingling with that steady dripping—a hum of movement, several pairs of feet creeping forward.

And drawing closer.

They were relentless. For a few moments there, Layne had thought he'd lost them.

No luck. They were close.

Layne dashed off, twisting his body to avoid a shaft of moonlight streaming through a shattered skylight.

While the facility was just another abandoned industrial relic on the outskirts of Plymouth, it served as a reminder of the city's heritage, a monumental heritage for a city its size—just 7,000 people, according to the last census in 1990.

It was such a random and forgotten place, this inoperational facility to which Layne had tracked the shipments by following the shipping manifests he'd stumbled upon.

The cheese manifests.

Now, this sprawling expanse of industrial neglect could end up where Layne died. That's what happened when you dug up things best left buried—things people were willing to kill for.

He leaned against the cold metal of a processing tank. His breaths were labored, shaky. He heard the footsteps again. The men were close.

His mind flashed on what had landed him here, to those damn manifests he'd found, should have left alone. The discrepancies. The connections he shouldn't have made.

At first, he hadn't seen the whole picture. Just knew it was big.

But how could he have?

Things like this didn't happen in small Wisconsin towns. They sure as hell didn't happen over *cheese*.

Or so he'd thought. Two months ago.

He'd learned a lot of hard lessons these last two months.

Layne kept himself steady, forcing his racing mind to the present. There was no time to wander in memories. His eyes cut through the darkness, looking for them. Movement caught his eye—shadows shifting a few yards away.

The men were there, closer than he'd thought.

His hand went to the pistol holstered at his side. He took it out, wrapped his shaking fingers around the handle. The thing was heavy. Damn heavy. Until a week ago, Layne had no clue guns weighed so much.

He'd bought it six days earlier at a shop in Milwaukee after he could no longer ignore his gut instincts screaming that the investigation had begun taking dark turns. The matte black metal felt alien in his grip—all that weight but also strange ridges and notches whose purposes he could only guess at.

His eyes narrowed, focusing on the subtle shift in the shadows. There! A figure moved, almost imperceptibly, but enough to notice. Chest thundering, Layne watched and waited to see if the shadow would move in his direction.

For a moment, it looked like the figure was heading for the door to the south...

...but then it pivoted, heading right for Layne.

Shit!

His heart rate spiked, breath shuddering again. He willed it steady. Layne had no training for this—no background in survival, no lessons in staying calm under pressure. But somehow, instinct had taken over—a deep, buried response wired into the human core. Primal. Older than fear itself.

Right now, that was all he had left.

He slipped behind a nearby column. The other man came forward. His silhouette was unreasonably close now, the details sharpening into focus—tall frame, broad shoulders, plodding boots. He wore a sweatshirt. A watch sparkled in the moonlight on his wrist.

Hand still shaking, Layne reached out, grabbed a loose rivet atop a pile of debris to his left. He tossed it. A few yards away, the rivet *tinked* on the concrete floor.

The other man stopped, head pivoting to the opposite direction, tuned on the sound.

And Layne took off.

He darted between machinery, slipping into the shadows. Lungs burning. Legs heavy. His footsteps echoed in the empty halls, as did those of the man he'd just seen—along with several other sets of footsteps coming in Layne's direction.

Layne's move with the rivet had been foolishly hopeful.

The processing floor was a tangled maze of equipment and dark alleys. Layne knew the layout well; he'd studied it for over an hour the previous day, preparing for tonight. He knew that the next turn to his right led to a hallway that was his only potential escape.

But when he turned, there was Tom Weiler.

Weiler swept his pistol back and forth.

But...

...he hadn't spotted Layne!

Weiler's stance was lazy. His eyes were vacant. He was one of the least trained men Layne was up against. Layne quickly assessed the glazed-over look in Weiler's eyes—the guy was probably thinking about the overtime he was missing at the plant or whatever mindless TV sitcom he'd rather be watching.

Then Weiler did something even more foolish—he moved off his position, drifting toward where he'd heard the others converging.

Layne had an escape route.

His heart leaped, and he bolted forward, crouching, hiding behind the geometric silhouettes of the machinery. The doorway that Weiler had revealed when he stepped away was just ahead. It was cracked open a few inches, moonlight coming into the facility, puddling on the cracked floor.

This was it. Layne *could* survive this.

He had a clear shot to—

A figure emerged, blocking his path.

Layne gasped.

The man was average height with a plain build—yet disproportionately intimidating. His baseball cap was grease-stained, pulled low over a hard, angular face and half concealing a pair of close-set, light blue eyes. Strands of red hair curled out from under the hat's brim. His beard matched —mostly. A few streaks of white cut through the rust.

But Layne's eyes were locked not on the man's face but his arms. Wrist to shoulder, both limbs were covered in thick, uneven scar tissue. Jagged. Twisted. Visible even in the dim light.

Layne took a step back. Then another. Turned. Tried a new direction.

No good. More figures emerged.

He spun around again.

Another dead end.

They were everywhere now—six of them, moving silently in a manner that further indicated their elite training. Weapons out and held at the ready.

Layne's pulse hammered fast and hard.

The other men weren't saying a word, just closing in.

Layne couldn't turn right, couldn't go backward.

He couldn't go *anywhere*.

He was being herded, driven back toward the center of the building. The other men were closing in, a tightening noose.

Instinct urged Layne to use his pistol. But he didn't. Because the others weren't shooting, only closing in. If they'd wanted to, they could have turned him to mush by now.

He glanced around, assessing his options. None. The circle was closing too tight, too fast. No way out.

Only one choice.

He slowly crouched, set his gun down, and lifted his hands.

The night was suddenly still. He heard the water again.

Drip.

Drip.

Drip.

The men stepped out of concealment, moving with quiet confidence. Predators closing in. Pistols up, steady, locked on Layne. Hard faces. Cold eyes.

There was Tom Weiler, looking more composed than he had a few moments earlier, inching forward with his compatriots. But Layne saw something else in Weiler's eyes—worry, maybe, or embarrassment at his near fumble.

Then, the scarred man stepped forward ahead of the others. Not fast, not slow—just deliberate. The other men adjusted, falling in line behind him.

As Layne watched the scarred man take his position of prominence, he felt it in his gut before his brain caught up. The shift in the group's language. The other individual's unspoken deference toward the scarred man.

This scarred guy wasn't just another hired gun.

He was the one running the show.

And just like that, Layne knew. Knew exactly who he was looking at—the man he'd been chasing all this time.

It was him!

Too bad he'd figured it out only now when it was too late.

Yes, people die for strange reasons.

Cheese, Layne thought. *I'm gonna die over some damn cheese.*

CHAPTER TWO

Pittsburgh, Pennsylvania
Two days later

Apartment doors weren't typically this difficult to break down.

And vigilante assassin Silence Jones knew a thing or two on the topic. He had kicked and rammed and shouldered his way through many an apartment door in his years in the field.

This door, however, was a heavy steel number in Pittsburgh's Strip District, a historic wholesale and produce hub. Once filled with warehouses that shipped goods, the Strip District had been reborn into a vibrant community of eclectic markets, loft apartments, and trendy restaurants. Many of the now-renovated industrial buildings still showcased the rugged elements of their former uses.

The stubborn door in front of Silence—and the thick brick walls surrounding it—were relics of an earlier era built to withstand far heavier assaults than Silence's big-ass foot. Three kicks and the damn thing had hardly even shuddered.

From inside, he heard shuffling and harsh, panicked whispers. Harvey King was in there, freaking out as cartel hitmen closed in.

And here was Silence, burning precious seconds trying to—

Whack!

Catching Silence by surprise, the door finally gave way, flying open and banging into the interior wall.

Silence half-stumbled inside to find Harvey—disheveled, wide-eyed, messenger bag clutched to his chest—backing away from his balcony as a dark figure fiddled with the window, which was open four inches. Another figure followed close behind.

Harvey's hands were shaking. Silence saw a small piece of folded white paper pinched between his fingers.

The loft apartment overflowed with industrial-chic potential: exposed brick walls, lofty ceilings with steel beams overhead, and tall windows. In a flash, Silence pictured what he would do with the place, draping it in his minimalist tastes—lots of black, white, gray; glass and stainless steel; a few oversized houseplants here and there to break up the monotone.

However, any trendy vibe had been stifled by Harvey's chaotic presence. Those tall windows that would have bathed the place in natural light were choked by thick curtains. Paperwork spilled from manila folders onto the hardwood floor. Stacks of dog-eared books teetered near an aging desk. A cheap futon in the corner, a card table in the other.

Silence had a clear sight line to the figure on the balcony, but he kept his finger away from the trigger. Firing through the window wasn't an option. He wasn't about to endanger innocent bystanders with an errant bullet or with shattered glass that would rain down on anyone passing on the sidewalk four floors below.

He sidestepped a scattered pile of newspapers and pulled

Harvey behind a hideous orange armchair that looked like it belonged in a late-1960s sitcom. Better than no cover at all.

Harvey clutched his messenger bag like a life preserver, breaths coming in erratic bursts as he tried to make himself as small as possible.

Harvey King...

Until about three seconds ago, Silence hadn't seen this guy in two years. He'd hoped to never see him again. But here Harvey was, squeezed right up against Silence's shoulder, shaking.

A normal person would be shaking in a situation like this, but Harvey was *always* shaking in some form or another, be it a tapping toe, a restless hand, or a lip being absentmindedly gnawed between his teeth. Constantly moving. Not out of nerves—though Harvey had plenty of those—but because he didn't know how to stop. Surplus energy incarnate.

In fitting with his twitchiness, Harvey's build was slight and wiry, amplified by his propensity to wear slightly oversized clothes. He would look like a hobo if he weren't so meticulously clean. Germophobia has its perks.

Harvey was in his late forties, white. Slightly hunched posture. Deep brown eyes, always a little too wide. Graying hair styled in the vein of Einstein or Eraserhead, like he'd just walked through a wind tunnel and never bothered to fix it.

Nervous. Intelligent. Paranoid.

And annoying as all hell.

The half-open window groaned. The first attacker swung a leg inside and paused to scan the room. The second man slid in behind him. Both were dressed in cargo pants and canvas jackets. Both were armed with a Taurus PT92.

They had yet to spot Silence and Harvey behind the unironically vintage armchair.

Pity.

Silence's Beretta 92FS barked once.

The first hitman's head snapped back, body crumpling. The second dove behind Harvey's kitchen island. And raised a weapon.

"Get down!" Silence growled, grabbing Harvey's collar and yanking him to the floor.

The words sent a shot of pain down Silence's throat. An incident years earlier had nearly killed Silence and left him with a permanently damaged larynx. Speaking was torturous to the mass of scar tissue in his neck. Yelling was even worse.

A burst of gunfire pounded into the brick wall behind where Harvey had been standing. Silence's ears rang. Harvey's mouth opened, and he squeaked—actually *squeaked*—then army-crawled toward his bathroom, still clutching that damn bag.

"You know what this reminds me of?" Harvey shouted. There was the sound of something knocking over—soap dish? Toothbrush holder? A crash of something heavier. "This supply chain management seminar I attended in Cleveland. Total chaos. Coffee machine broke, schedule got jumbled."

Silence slid into the bathroom next to Harvey. The space was cramped. Antique hexagonal tile. Original sink and toilet. Clawfoot tub.

He leaned toward the doorway, tried to listen for the other man in the loft's main space beyond.

But Harvey was still talking.

"Then this guy, some intern, tries to set up the projector and somehow trips over the catering table," Harvey said. "Lasagna, everywhere. People screaming. The CEO panics, starts running—like, full sprint—for no reason, knocks over a giant banner, which drops straight onto a tray of live lobsters—"

"Shut up, Harvey!" Silence growled. More pain in his throat.

Movement.

At the orange chair.

The hitman popped up, weapon swinging to the left. Silence was faster. Two rounds through the chair. Stuffing erupted. The chair kicked back eight inches. Harvey screamed. Blood splattered on brick, and the man collapsed.

More footsteps in the hall. Heavy footsteps. Could be neighbors.

But the noise was more likely additional hitmen.

"Time to go," Silence said and swallowed.

Frequent swallowing was a technique he used to ease the torment in his throat.

Harvey wiggled past him, making a beeline for the opposite side of the loft before Silence grabbed his arm.

"No!" Harvey said. "I wasn't able to get Mitsy before the guys showed up at the windows!"

Silence frowned. "Dog? Cat?"

"Air plant."

Harvey pointed frantically. Silence followed the motion.

A tiny, spiky green thing sat in a thumb-sized blue porcelain dish-magnet, stuck dead-center on the refrigerator door.

Silence blinked.

Then he looked at the windows. The door. The sound of footsteps closing in.

He growled, ran to the kitchen area, ripped the plant-magnet from the fridge, and shoved it into his pocket.

"Careful with her!" Harvey yelped.

Silence grabbed Harvey's arm again and dragged him toward the door. Harvey stumbled, knocked over a chair, nearly face-planted. His messenger bag swung wildly.

They hit the hallway as boots thundered up the stairwell. But Silence had studied the building's layout from the schematics included in his mission materials—if this damn fool's errand could even be classified as a "mission." He pulled Harvey toward the old freight elevator instead of the stairs.

The elevator's gate squealed as Silence yanked it aside. He shoved Harvey in, followed, and went for the control panel...

...but was stopped.

A figure appeared in the gap as the gate was closing. Muscled arms forced the gate back open and clawed at Silence's chest.

Silence's palm strike caught the man's throat. The hitman gagged, hands going to his neck, momentarily stunned.

And Silence seized upon this moment of paralysis, noticing a gruesome opportunity: a way to snap the man in two.

He grabbed the other man's jacket, reached past him to the elevator's control panel, and stabbed a finger into the 1 button.

Unfortunately for the man in his grip, this elevator was ancient, and safety features weren't quite the same as modern standards.

The elevator car shuddered into motion. Silence had the guy trapped now between the car and the floor.

The hitman's eyes widened as he realized his position, but Silence held firm on the guy's jacket. Brutal training and years of field experience had given Silence relentless, mechanical strength. This dude wasn't going anywhere.

The car lurched, continued descending.

The hitman thrashed, trying to pull himself entirely into the car.

Too late.

A wet crunch filled the shaft as the elevator car met the next floor's edge. The hitman's struggles ceased. What remained of him dragged along the shaft wall as they descended.

Silence let go, and the limp form lifted away, shaking the car violently. Silence and Harvey both reached out to the walls to catch their balance. Blood dripped onto the steel floor.

Harvey dry-heaved in the corner.

The elevator came to a halt on the ground floor. The doors groaned open to reveal a sprawling lobby.

It was a fusion of old industry and modern chic, perfectly curated. Exposed brick walls. Steel beams left raw and unpolished. Asymmetric clusters of pendant lights dangling from above, casting pools of light on polished concrete floors. Leather armchairs and sofas. A sleek concierge desk near the entrance.

Silence stepped forward, scanning the open space. Quiet. For now.

The only sign of life was the security camera on the wall behind the concierge desk, red light blinking. Silence suspected someone might be on the other side of the closed door beneath it, perhaps on a break.

He nudged Harvey forward. "Stay behind..." he said and swallowed. "Me."

They moved across the space, footsteps tapping. Silence kept their pace hurried but not attention-grabbing, minding the security camera. They were yards away from the glass revolving doors.

Then he heard it. The echo of footsteps—rushed, coordinated.

The stairwell team had caught up.

The door to the stairwell burst open, and two hostiles emerged, fanning out. Weapons up. Muzzles flared.

Crack! Crack! Crack!

Silence shoved Harvey behind a steel column and returned fire in a blur of movement—up, across. Two precise shots. Two bodies hitting polished concrete.

Surely dead, both of them. But Silence didn't trust the feeling. Instinct was good; certainty was better.

He stepped away from Harvey, Beretta at the ready, eyes scanning.

"Where are you going?" Harvey hissed, still crouched behind the column. "Don't leave me!"

Silence ignored him. He had to be sure.

He reached the first body—eyes wide, frozen in the last moment of life. Silence leveled his pistol, put two rounds in the guy's head. The sound cracked through the cavernous lobby.

Then he moved to the second man. Same treatment, a pair of shots to the head.

Double-taps. The only way to be sure.

The lobby was quiet again.

He turned back to Harvey, who was bear-hugging his messenger bag.

"Let's roll," Silence said and grabbed Harvey's jacket, yanked him up.

One more glance at the blinking red security light. The concierge desk was still empty. Could mean the place was unstaffed—it was 10 in the morning on a Sunday, after all—or maybe the concierge had the good sense to stay out of sight after a gunfight broke out in the lobby. Either scenario made sense.

They pushed through the revolving door and out onto the street. Silence's silver Cadillac Seville STS was parked at the curb, wedged between a rusted pickup and an Accord. Traffic crawled past—morning commuters, delivery vans, the occasional cab blasting its horn. A city bus sighed to a stop half a block away, brakes hissing. Pedestrians moved along the sidewalk.

Silence opened the passenger door, shoved Harvey into the seat, then circled the car and slid behind the wheel. The engine roared to life, tires chirped, and they were off.

As they peeled through the Strip District, Harvey

clutched his messenger bag. The bag contained evidence of cartel operations—invoices, bank records—enough to take down their entire East Coast network. The Watchers, Silence's employers, had been right; Harvey needed protection.

Silence checked his rearview. Empty street behind them. In the distance, blue lights. They'd left just in time.

He dug in his pocket, retrieved Mitsy, and reached the tiny plant across the center console to the passenger seat. Harvey received it eagerly, cupping Mitsy with both hands and speaking a few kind words before dropping the plant in his own jacket pocket—the left breast pocket—and giving it a little pat.

"That was... that was..." Harvey's voice shook. He took a deep breath, then launched into nervous chatter. "I mean, I knew they'd come eventually, but I didn't think—when they started coming through the balcony, I almost—and then you just—and that guy in the elevator—"

"Harvey... relax," Silence said.

Harvey fell silent. For about three seconds.

"Where are we going? They'll follow us, won't they? They always follow in movies. Do you have a plan? You must have a plan. Your people always have a—"

"*Harvey.*"

"Right. Sorry. Quiet. I'll be quiet." His hands were moving rapidly, fiddling with that folded piece of paper.

Silence tensed, knowing the next outburst was only moments away.

It was going to be a long drive to California.

CHAPTER THREE

Plymouth, Wisconsin

JOANNE DALEY WAS TRYING to stay open-minded and kind-hearted.

But the place was called The Mullet.

She was struggling not to slip into her past tendencies toward condescension.

The afternoon sun hit the building hard, dragging every flaw into the open—peeling paint, rust stains creeping down from the gutters, a flickering neon sign missing half its letters. Sandwiched between a defunct video store and a discount furniture outlet, the place exuded the kind of seediness that would have once made her cross the street, nose in the air.

She almost laughed at the name—The Mullet. This bar was nowhere near an ocean and sat a good twenty minutes inland from Lake Michigan. Did mullet fish even swim in the Great Lakes? She had no clue. But there was little doubt in her mind that the name had nothing to do with fish; it was about the haircut.

The mullet—a hairstyle mocked and embraced in equal

measure, a badge of both ridicule and pride for low-class culture.

The old Joanne would have had a lot to say about The Mullet. She would have pulled students aside if she knew their parents frequented places like this, gently suggesting that such distasteful associations could affect the students' futures.

Never in a million years would she have imagined she'd be sitting outside such an establishment, debating whether to step inside.

But here she was, white-knuckling the steering wheel of her rental car, staring at The Mullet's dented steel doors, trying to summon the nerve to approach them.

Karma had a twisted sense of humor.

She reached into her purse and extracted the envelope, handling it carefully, like a museum piece—though its bent corners and creases showed she'd already put it through plenty. Her address back in Morro Bay was centered on the front in Layne Grosicki's small, precise handwriting.

She didn't need to reread the letter. Every word was seared into her memory.

But she unfolded it anyway. Maybe to remind herself why she was here, the importance of this self-imposed duty. Maybe to steel herself before stepping inside the bar.

Or maybe just to stall some more.

Dear Mrs. Daley,

It might be strange, after all this time, to receive this letter. You might remember me—Layne Grosicki, kindergarten student, 30 years ago. I've carried pieces of that classroom with me my whole life, for better or worse, and I need your help now in a way I never thought I would.

I want to start by saying I've come to understand that people are complicated. You were, and maybe still are, a complicated person. The way you made me wear that "Speak Clearly" headband—

She abruptly stopped reading. Had to.

Her fingers lingered on the paper's edge momentarily before she forced herself to refold it.

If only there were a way for her to glean a clue from the obfuscated text, some hint about what had driven Layne to his death...

But no. She'd read it so many times she had every word memorized, and she *still* didn't understand the hidden message. It was beyond her grasp.

There was only one person who could figure out the true meaning.

The problem was, that person was unreachable.

That was why Joanne found herself in Wisconsin, of all places, trying to gather the courage to step outside and enter a seedy bar called The Mullet.

A motorcycle rumbled into the parking lot, its helmet-less rider wearing the precise kind of haircut the bar's name celebrated. The man dismounted, adjusted his crotch, and strode inside without a backward glance.

Joanne took a deep breath and released her chokehold on the steering wheel.

Come on, you old bitch, she thought. *You've faced down innumerable bratty five-year-olds. You can handle this place.*

It was a wild exaggeration, and she knew it.

Nevertheless, she got out of the car.

The parking lot was ruinous, riddled with potholes. A chill hung in the air—not quite cold, but enough to make her wrap her arms around herself. Overhead, the neon sign buzzed.

After another moment's hesitation at the dented doors, she entered.

Inside, The Mullet looked exactly as she had expected. Darker than necessary, air thick with stale beer and cigarette smoke, the latter of which probably dated to the Reagan administration. A handful of afternoon regulars hunched over their drinks, all turning to stare as she entered.

Her hands balled into fists at her sides, but Joanne pushed on, spine straight, chin up—the posture that had commanded respect from generations of kindergarteners felt useless here, armor made of tissue paper.

Behind the bar, a hard-faced woman with faded tattoos looked her over—brief, dismissive.

"What'll it be?" Her voice was rough, the vocal equivalent of the beer-and-cigarette stench in the air.

"White wine?" Joanne said. She wasn't sure why it came out like a question, but she regretted it instantly. Made her sound uncertain. Weak.

The other woman snorted, gave Joanne a slow once-over. "Beer or liquor, sweetheart. This ain't your country club."

Joanne hardly looked country club-ready. Light sweater, green slacks, flats. Nothing particularly fancy.

"Beer, then. Whatever's on tap."

The beer appeared quickly, foam slopping over the sides. Joanne pulled it closer but didn't drink. Instead, she reached into her purse and took out a folded sheet of computer paper —an image she'd printed from the Internet.

"I'm looking for information about this man." She kept her voice steady, teacher-firm. "Layne Grosicki. I heard he came through here a time or two during the last couple of weeks."

As the bartender looked up from the image, her eyes flickered with something—recognition?—before narrowing. "Maybe. What's it to you?"

Hope fluttered in Joanne's chest. She pressed on. "He's

dead. I'm trying to understand why. If you know anything—" She pulled out her wallet. "I can make it worth your time."

The woman's lips curved into a cruel smile. "Oh honey, I'm just screwing with you. I don't know your dead guy, and I don't give a shit about him. Don't be so naive." She leaned closer. "You're lucky I'm so damn nice. Somebody else would've taken you for every dollar in that wallet, fed you whatever story you wanted to hear. Now get out, old bat. You don't belong here."

The words hit hard. Joanne's chest tightened as laughter rippled from the regulars at the bar. They'd been watching, all of them, she realized. Enjoying the show.

Joanne glanced at the beer. Then, the bartender. Then, the man at the nearest table laughing at her. He was the man who'd come in just before her. The motorcyclist. The guy with the mullet haircut.

A fresh wave of patrons pushed through the door, all wearing gray coveralls—shift change at some nearby factory, perhaps. The distraction was all she needed.

Joanne stood, smoothed her slacks with trembling hands. Walked out, head high, ignoring the mockery that followed her.

She made it inside the car before the shaking really hit.

A moment to breathe, then she folded the computer-printed image and slid it back into her purse, where it came to rest beside Layne's letter. For a moment, her eyes lingered on the envelope. She snapped the purse shut.

Another dead end. Another humiliation.

She was a retired schoolteacher from California, for heaven's sake. What was she doing here, poking into dark corners, chasing answers about a death that every official report called an accident?

Foolishness, thy name is Joanne.

But she knew this was the right thing. She wasn't just

correcting a mistake that had slipped past law enforcement—she was making amends.

And she would keep going. No matter how many doors slammed in her face.

Joanne started the car, hands steadier now.

Once upon a time, she'd been cruel. A real bitch. Wielding words like weapons against people who couldn't fight back.

Perhaps this really was karma and its twisted sense of humor—all these doors closing, all these hostile faces.

But Joanne wasn't the woman she had been in the past. And she wasn't leaving Plymouth, Wisconsin, until she found the truth, no matter how often she was laughed out of places like The Mullet.

She pulled out of the parking lot.

CHAPTER FOUR

Julian McCrorie hated this place.

He hated the damp, the rot, the way the air clung to his skin like something living. The entire place—every room, every half-collapsed hallway—smelled like a mix of mildew and old milk, pungent and sour.

Maybe it was illogical to think he smelled milk. The plant had been shut down for decades; any trace of dairy was long gone. Perhaps, then, it was McCrorie's subconscious playing tricks on him, filling in the gaps with what he knew of the abandoned location's former lot in life.

Either way, the place stank.

The floor was a maze of cracked concrete and rusted metal, slick with who-knew-what. He could hear the rats, always just beyond the edge of the light, scratching at the walls, darting through shadows.

The worst part of it was the quiet.

But it wasn't *true* quiet—McCrorie understood that type of quiet, thrived in it. True quiet was calm, steady. This, though, was the type of quiet that made you listen too hard and second-guess what was lurking in the dark. The type that toyed with you.

The last several days, however, McCrorie would've welcomed the quiet during his visits to the plant.

Because the alternative was worse—the noises from the man deep in the structure, way down in the shadows.

Sometimes, he yelled. Sometimes, he screamed. Sometimes, he banged on the metal, over and over.

McCrorie had even heard the man cry. Multiple times.

Right now, he was banging again.

Bang. Bang. Bang.

Slow and steady, like some ghoul, something out of an old ghost movie.

Distant. Hollow. Almost... mournful.

McCrorie tried his best to ignore it.

He pulled his coat tighter against the night's chill, stepped deeper into the skeleton of the old processing plant.

His men spread out, phantoms in the ruins. These were the same guys who tracked down Layne Grosicki two days earlier at this very location—good, solid men. They knew how to work together, knew how to do what had to be done.

That's why McCrorie had picked them. Loyalty was everything in McCrorie's line of work. And tonight, his men's loyalty was going to be tested.

Because their target was one of their own.

Tom Weiler.

A fool. A liability.

Two days ago, Weiler was here in the plant with them, helping corner Layne Grosicki.

But Weiler had made a mistake, dropped his guard, and McCrorie had had to correct the error, cutting off Grosicki's path just before the guy could escape.

After that, Weiler had disappeared.

Disappearing meant a guy had something to hide. Disappearing was a problem.

And McCrorie didn't like problems.

Weiler had skipped work for two days. And his girlfriend hadn't seen him, hadn't been able to reach him.

McCrorie dispatched his men throughout the Plymouth area, and within forty-eight hours, they had Weiler cornered —right back where it started, at the crumbling processing plant on the edge of town.

Since the plant was the base of operations, maybe Weiler thought he was being clever. Maybe he figured McCrorie would never look for him here.

He was wrong.

McCrorie's back tensed as he ducked beneath a corroded pipe. A too-familiar, too-constant pang flared along his left arm, deep beneath the layers of scar tissue. Old damage, long healed but never forgotten. The burned skin pulled tight when he moved a certain way, a permanent reminder of the night that had shaped him.

He ignored it. His body was a machine—years of discipline carved into muscle and precision. He could handle himself.

Another few steps forward, and he paused. Something felt off.

The place was *too* quiet...

With a flick of his fingers, his men also halted. They listened.

McCrorie sifted through the sounds—the groaning of the old plant as the wind pushed against it, the distant tap of water dripping onto metal, the scurry of rodents in the debris.

And the soul in the depths of the structure, banging on the walls—*Bang. Bang. Bang.*

And...

There.

Footsteps.

Weiler was close.

McCrorie grinned. Relief.

He took off, leading the charge, moving deeper into the labyrinth of rust and decay. His boots landed light, barely stirring the dust. They closed in, weaving between the hulking remnants of old machinery and broken conveyor belts.

Ahead, a storage room. The door was cracked open.

McCrorie lifted a fist. His men stopped.

He stepped inside.

The room was an esoteric graveyard—barrels stacked high, a mound of shattered dairy bottles, and the remnants of abandoned equipment strewn across the floor. And there, tucked behind a crate in the far corner, Weiler.

A flicker of movement gave the guy away—a quick flash of moonlight on his face before the shadows swallowed him again.

McCrorie sighed. Pathetic.

He adjusted his ball cap and ran a hand over his beard. "Hey, Weiler," he called softly. "Why don't you come out of there?"

No response.

Weiler peeked over the top of the crate. Wide eyes. Wet lips. The guy was a cornered rat, all twitchy and desperate.

"I—I..."

McCrorie's men shifted around the room, closing in.

"I said *come out*," McCrorie said, his words echoing off the surroundings, losing all its moments-earlier faux kindness.

Weiler hesitated, then slowly rose to his feet. He looked at the others, their weapons held low but ready. He swallowed hard.

This guy had once been one of them. Now he looked like

a ghost, all sweat and panic, his shirt torn, his hands shaking. Weiler knew what was coming.

McCrorie stepped closer, stopping just twenty feet away. Close enough for Weiler to see the certainty in his eyes.

"You screwed up," he said. "That was bad enough. But tell me, why'd you go on the run for two days?"

Weiler licked his lips. Looked at the others, then the rusted beams above, like there was an escape route hidden somewhere up there in the rot.

"I... I couldn't do it," he stammered. "The deal... It isn't just wrong, Mr. McCrorie. It's suicidal. I'm trying to save you! Save all of us. There're people watching. I seen 'em! The other day, I—"

"Oh, shut up!"

This display was pathetic enough. Weiler didn't need to make it worse with pointless lying.

"I swear!" Weiler's voice cracked. "They've been tailing me! I—I tried to lose them, but I had to run. I did it for all of us. You don't see it, but they're coming for you."

McCrorie tilted his head. Held Weiler's gaze. Let the quiet stretch.

Then he nodded. Like he understood. Like he believed.

"You think you're some kind of savior, huh?" McCrorie's voice was soft again, almost amused. "That's cute."

Weiler took a step forward, hopeful.

Then McCrorie's face hardened. "But you know what I think? I think you're a coward."

Weiler's mouth opened—one last protest, one last plea. But McCrorie raised a hand.

"That's your final mistake."

A flick of his wrist.

His men moved.

Weiler barely had time to gasp before they grabbed him and dragged him toward a stack of rusted crates. Someone pulled a length of wire from the debris, twisting it around Weiler's wrists and tying him to a beam.

McCrorie watched, impassive.

Another of his men uncoiled the end of a chain threaded through a corroded metal panel in the wall, its other end extending toward the ceiling. A sharp tug sent the chain free. It didn't move fast, but it didn't have to. The weight alone did the work.

The chain rattled as it plunged downward. Weiler barely got out half a scream before it slammed into his chest. A dull, sickening crunch. His legs buckled. The breath left him in a wheezing gasp as he crumpled to the floor.

The chain coiled into a three-foot mound. When it stilled, the only portion of Weiler still visible was the lower half of the man's left leg.

Then, there was just the creak of the old plant settling and the last echoes of the impact fading into nothing.

And the distant *bang, bang, bang.*

McCrorie didn't flinch. He pulled a cigarette from his coat pocket, lit it, and turned away.

The job was done.

But deep down, he knew this wasn't over.

First Grosicki. Now Weiler. A pattern was forming.

A problem.

McCrorie didn't like problems.

And if there was one thing he knew about problems, it was that you had to cut them out before they spread.

CHAPTER FIVE

Montrose, Illinois

FOUR STATES.

Trapped in the Cadillac, Silence had endured Harvey's constant chatter *in four different states.*

Through Pennsylvania's rolling hills, where Harvey had detailed the complete shipping history of every truck stop they passed by. Past Ohio's endless cornfields, during which Harvey lectured on agricultural transport logistics. Through forests and more cornfields in Indiana, where Silence was treated to an exhaustive analysis of interstate weight station protocols.

And now, an hour into Illinois, where more corn stretched to the horizon on all sides of Interstate 70 as the Cadillac pushed farther west. Silence was hurtling along at over seventy miles per hour, yet he still couldn't outrun his plight. He was trapped.

Usually, the open road was Silence's happy place, especially interstate highways. He loved road trips, always had. Nothing else made him feel as free and, thus, happy.

But not this time.

Not with Harvey.

He strangled the steering wheel with both hands.

"So I've been thinking about rest stop efficiency," Harvey said, using both hands to fold a McDonald's receipt, making it smaller and smaller. "If we calculate average bladder capacity against fluid intake rates, factoring in seasonal temperature variations that affect hydration needs..."

Silence's jaw clenched. The man hadn't stopped talking since Pittsburgh. Not for a single blessed moment. Not even during the single-hour nap Silence had taken at a rest area somewhere in Ohio, where Harvey had even invaded his dreams, a disassociated version of him rambling about proper invoice filings.

"Did you know the first modern highway rest area was built in 1958, Rex?" Harvey rattled on, still working on the McDonald's receipt, sharpening the folds.

Harvey had called Silence "Rex," the name Silence had given him two years ago when they met during Silence's Pittsburgh assignment. As a security precaution, Silence gave everyone to whom he offered his services an alias. He always chose a one-syllable name to lower the number of syllables he needed to run through his ruined throat. The effect was minuscule but helpful.

"Though technically," Harvey continued, "there's another way of looking at it. If you count primitive waypoints used by..."

A vigilante assassin. That's what Silence was. The Watchers' top operator. Silence had dismantled terrorist cells. Eliminated cartel kingpins. Thwarted biological attacks. His name —or rather, his rumored names, of which there were many urban legends—inspired fear in the criminal underworld.

And now he was playing chauffeur.

Among the techniques utilized by the Watchers—a covert

group operating within U.S. government to correct injustices and punish those who had escaped procedural justice—assassinations were their usual method of evening the scales.

But not always.

Sometimes, there was other work to be done. Occasionally, the Watchers handled their own version of witness relocation.

That was the treatment Harvey King was receiving—new name, new home, new life on the other side of the country.

Silence was an Asset, the term for the Watchers' field agents, their assassins. But right now, his job was entirely different: *Driving Miss Daisy*-ing Harvey from Pennsylvania to California so the man could begin his new life.

Two years earlier, Harvey had gotten himself tangled in cartel business. The Watchers had dispatched Silence to Pittsburgh to clean up the mess, which he did. Effectively. For twenty-six months, the Watchers assumed Harvey was in the clear.

Then, the situation shifted. Quickly. Drastically.

It was decided that Harvey needed to disappear.

Flying wasn't an option—Harvey hated it, and security risks were too high. The cartel chasing him wasn't some low-level operation; they were shockingly sophisticated in cyber-crime, capable of tracking airline records, public and private.

And since Silence was the one who had saved Harvey the first time, he was the one assigned this miserable task.

So here he was...

The Cadillac's engine hummed as they crossed yet another cornfield. Harvey had already reorganized the glove compartment twice, arranged all the gas receipts by ZIP code, and alphabetized the road maps. He'd even color-coded the fast food wrappers before disposing them in separate bags.

"—which reminds me," Harvey was saying, "we should

organize the glove compartment again. I have a system that—"

"You just did..." Silence said and swallowed. "That. An hour ago!"

Silence was about to swallow again and really give it to Harvey, but a voice spoke to him in his mind, cutting him off.

Easy, love, C.C. said. *Be kind. He's a sweet man.*

He's a jackass! Silence replied.

Love!

C.C. was Silence's deceased fiancée. Murdered. Years ago. An internalized version of her often spoke to Silence in his mind. In life, she'd been wise well beyond her years, and Silence relied on that wisdom even after her death.

She spoke to him during times of high stress, which were frequent in Silence's line of work as a vigilante assassin.

Bullets. Injuries. Grueling choices. Certain death.

And, in this case, a patience-testing blabbermouth...

Harvey was talking again. But this time, not to Silence. Mitsy, the air plant, sat cupped in his hands. Silence couldn't make out what was being said, but it was a steady stream of love-filled consciousness, as persistent as any of Harvey's other ramblings.

Silence's cellular phone buzzed. He'd never been so grateful for an interruption.

Until he saw the number.

Doc Hazel.

Shit.

Doc Hazel... the Watchers' idea of mandatory mental health counseling. Silence had never asked for it. Never wanted it. But his employers didn't care.

Professionally speaking, Silence had no clue what Doc Hazel actually was. She'd never offered a title or credentials. So, he didn't know if she was a psychologist, a psychiatrist, or some kind of counselor.

In fact, he'd come to suspect that she was none of the above. There were strong indicators that she was merely *playing* the part of a mental health professional. Acting.

Still, over time, Doc Hazel had become a fixture. One of the few constants in a life built on change. Reliable. Unshakable. Always there, whether Silence liked it or not.

He flipped the phone open. "Ma'am?"

"Good morning, Suppressor." Doc Hazel's clinical tone was as robotic as ever.

Suppressor was Silence's codename. He also had the numerical title Asset 23, or A-23 for short.

"How's the transport proceeding?" Doc Hazel continued.

"Fine."

In the passenger seat, Harvey was now sorting sugar packets into neat piles based on what appeared to be granule size.

"Can we do my session..." Silence said and swallowed. "Now? Over the phone?"

He was referring to their mental health sessions—traditional lie-down-and-tell-me-about-your-feelings affairs, which were typically held in person but sometimes over the phone—and he'd asked her hopefully.

Perhaps too hopefully.

A pause from the other end of the line. A long one.

Then, finally, Doc Hazel spoke. "I'm sorry... did you just ask for a session?" Her voice carried genuine incredulity—a momentary crack in the facade of her robot act—like she'd just been told the sky had turned green. "You hate our sessions, Suppressor. Actively. Passionately. I once offered you a double session, and you looked like I'd suggested self-immolation."

Silence didn't respond. He waited.

"No, we're not doing your session over the phone," Doc Hazel said. A brief pause, then her voice leveled out, back to business. "I've got something different for you this time in lieu of our normal session. A replacement exercise." Another beat. "But that's not why I'm calling. This is about Wisconsin."

Silence frowned. "Wisconsin?"

"You have an additional assignment there. A brief detour."

It took Silence a moment.

"Already on assignment," he said and swallowed. "Transporting a guy cross-country."

He glanced at the passenger seat. Harvey was tidying the stacks of sugar packets. He looked up from his work, smiled at Silence.

Silence turned his attention back to the road.

"I'm well aware," Doc Hazel snapped. "This is a simple matter. Retired kindergarten teacher, Joanne Daley, seventy-four, is investigating a former student's death. Local authorities have deemed it an accident, but she persists. We need you to... provide clarity. Then send her home to California."

Silence's frown deepened. California. Where he was taking Harvey.

Surely they weren't expecting him to chauffeur *two* people...

"But, I have..." Silence said, swallowed. "A protectee."

As much as Harvey annoyed Silence, he didn't want to put Harvey in danger.

And he sure as hell didn't want a repeat of what had happened during the mission two years ago—Harvey tripping over himself, getting in the way at every turn.

"This wouldn't typically be an Asset assignment," Doc Hazel said.

Ah... now Silence understood.

"A Green..." he said and swallowed. "Assignment?"

"Correct."

A Green Assignment—the Watchers' term for a nonviolent operation. Something quiet. Low risk. The kind of job they usually handed to Specialists, not Assets.

Specialists—a higher rank in the Watchers' structure—handled logistics, intelligence, and infiltration. Assets handled elimination.

The Watchers were sending Silence in on a damn Green! Wasting more of his time. He was already babysitting Harvey, and now he was tasked with some low-risk intel job, something an unarmed Specialist could handle with a clipboard and a cup of coffee.

No real danger, no real work. Just a detour from an already demeaning assignment. A distraction upon a distraction.

Silence exhaled sharply.

Doc Hazel didn't wait for him to object.

"Resources are stretched thin right now, Suppressor," she said. "We don't have the Specialist personnel to spare, and you're already on the road. You're in the vague vicinity—only six hours south of Plymouth, Wisconsin—which makes you the closest available Asset. It's simple logistics."

"*Only* six hours?" His ruined throat suddenly felt even rawer. He swallowed.

"The situation requires delicate handling," Doc Hazel said. "Ms. Daley might not be entirely stable. She somehow got wind of the former student's—Layne Grosicki's—death in Wisconsin and flew across the country to investigate."

Silence frowned. "And?"

"And from what we've seen, Grosicki—who worked as an accountant in Milwaukee for a company called HarborGate Logistics—got it in his head that something shady was happening with shipping manifests. Repeated discrepancies, numbers that didn't add up. He started poking around, convinced that artisanal cheese shipments were being used for something nefarious. But there's no evidence of that. He played Colombo in Plymouth and ended up having an accident."

"What kind?"

"Fell from a loading dock late at night. Blunt force trauma. Coroner's report fully supports it," Doc Hazel said. "We think Ms. Daley feels responsible somehow. Like she owes it to her former student to figure this out. School records from Morro Bay, California, indicate she received multiple complaints from parents over the years. Nothing... extreme. No reports of abuse or anything. But apparently she was a mean, unsympathetic bitch."

"To... kindergarteners?"

"Kindergarteners."

Ugh. Silence disliked the woman already.

"Given her age, the fact that there's nothing to indicate foul play in Grosicki's death, and the fact that she flew across the country and is apparently knocking on every door in the city of Plymouth, refusing to leave, we suspect she may be suffering from early, undiagnosed symptoms of dementia. The mission materials are waiting in your email," Doc Hazel said. "Reports, photos, statements. Use them to walk Ms. Daley through the facts, show her there's nothing to chase. Then, convince her to go back to California."

She let that hang for a moment. Then came the inevitable twist. "Now, since you were so eager for our counseling session, let's go over the alternative therapy task I'm assigning you." Smug satisfaction oozed through the speaker.

Silence strangled the steering wheel some more.

"Instead of our usual session, you'll complete an exercise designed to enhance emotional reflection and improve operational clarity," Doc Hazel said.

Silence blinked.

"You're with Harvey King," Doc Hazel continued. "Transporting the man across the country, a man whose life you impacted two years earlier. This is the perfect opportunity for you to reflect upon the ways in which we all affect one another, Suppressor."

Next to Silence, Harvey had started humming softly, abandoning his original sugar packet arrangement. Now, he was building a spiral, carefully adjusting each packet for perfect angular alignment, pausing every few seconds to check his work.

"You'll be writing letters. Three of them," Doc Hazel said. "One to someone you've wronged. One to someone who wronged you. And one to someone whose life you impacted in an unexpected way. Don't worry—you won't be sending them. This is about you, not them. It's about understanding the ripple effects of your actions. Essential for someone in your position. And especially relevant, considering the company you're currently keeping."

Silence felt suddenly tense. His eyes flashed to Harvey. "Ma'am, I—"

"Consider how your choices affect others, Suppressor. Like ripples in a pond, spreading outward, touching distant shores we never see."

"But—"

"This is a directive, not a suggestion." Her tone left no room for argument. "I'll expect updates on your progress. The first letter should be completed within twenty-four hours."

"Ma'am, there's—"

"Now, you and Harvey have fun in Wisconsin." Dripping sarcasm. "Good luck, Suppressor."

Beep.

The line went dead.

Silence collapsed the phone. Beside him, Harvey had somehow acquired more sugar packets and was now expanding the spiral design on his lap to something akin to an elaborate mandala pattern.

He thought about the nature of the activity Doc Hazel had assigned, thought about what she'd said—*Consider how your choices affect others, Suppressor. Like ripples in a pond, spreading outward, touching distant shores we never see.*

Silence's jaw clenched. He believed in the butterfly effect and the ripple effect, of course, but he didn't think people should be held accountable to them. The world was too messy for that kind of thinking. Actions had consequences, sure, but not every tiny misstep deserved scrutiny, not every choice should be dragged up and examined under a microscope.

People made mistakes. Others who were impacted by those mistakes needed to accept that human beings were fallible and move on with their lives.

Demanding accountability for every minor failure and small infraction was preposterous. Life wasn't a ledger to be balanced.

And yet, there were people like Harvey. The man was an endless, nervous wreck of past grievances and perceived slights, haunted by things Silence would have written off and never thought about again. Maybe that was what Doc Hazel was getting at.

"Hey, Rex?" Harvey said, carefully placing another packet. "About those rest stops—I've been analyzing our route on these maps, and I've identified optimal stopping points based on facility cleanliness ratings, average user traffic patterns, and—did you know that some rest areas in Montana still use septic systems from the 1960s? Which reminds me of this fascinating article I read about wastewater treatment innovations in..."

This time, Silence's grip didn't tighten on the steering wheel. It slackened, fingers going limp as he let out a long exhale.

Resigned defeat.

Wisconsin. A Green Assignment. A six-hour detour. And still hundreds of miles to go.

With Harvey King.

He glanced at his passenger, who was now sketching a detailed diagram of his proposed rest stop optimization strategy on the back of the McDonald's receipt, which he'd unfolded and flattened against his thigh.

"—and if we factor in the seasonal migration patterns of long-haul truckers," Harvey continued, pulling out a small calculator, "we can predict peak usage times with a margin of error of only..."

Silence considered, briefly, jumping out the window.

Stop being so dramatic, love, C.C. said.

Silence exhaled.

Instead of jumping out the window, he pressed harder on the accelerator. The sooner they reached Wisconsin, the sooner he could get this Green Assignment over with, even if it was just convincing some old lady to stop being nosy and go home.

As he thought about it, maybe it wouldn't be such a bad thing if this Joanne Daley woman joined them in the car ride across the country.

It would sure as hell be better than enduring Harvey alone.

Harvey pulled out a fresh stack of handwritten notes. "Now, about this quaternary classification system I mentioned earlier..."

CHAPTER SIX

Plymouth, Wisconsin
Six long hours later

THE OUTSKIRTS OF PLYMOUTH, Wisconsin, rolled past the Cadillac, an image of picture-perfect small-town Americana that Silence had seen a thousand times before in a thousand different places. But like all the others, this little city had its own quirks, its own quiet sense of pride.

Harvey, for once, was silent, splitting his attention between the new town outside and the activity on his lap—fidgeting with a Shell station receipt, pinching the folds.

And for a moment, Silence felt that gentle, peaceful thrill—life on the road, laying eyes on a place he'd never seen. He settled a little deeper into the Cadillac's leather seat.

He liked this car. Liked it a lot. Hell, he loved it. But it hadn't been with him long. And it wouldn't be around for much longer, either. Every six months, the Watchers provided Silence a new set of wheels, whether he wanted them or not. So, Silence tried not to become overly attached to his vehicles, but he was often unsuccessful.

An arch stretched over the street ahead, declaring Plymouth as "THE CHEESE CAPITAL OF THE WORLD."

Silence grinned.

Another one of those places.

Like the Rhubarb Pie Capital of the World—Sumner, Washington. Or the Tenderloin Capital of the World—St. Joseph, Missouri. He'd passed through dozens of them, each proudly claiming its own peculiar and niche slice of global dominance.

But to claim oneself the *cheese* capital of the world was a tall boast indeed.

The Cadillac cruised past rows of brick buildings, solid and well-kept. Cheese shops everywhere. Every block had one, their windows crammed with wheels and wedges in every imaginable variety. Even the air smelled like it—sharp, aged, unmistakable. A town that didn't just make cheese. It lived it.

Beside him, Harvey's fingers were hard at work with the Shell receipt. As he looked closer, Silence saw Harvey folding the paper into a triangular shape. With maddening precision. Fold. Crease. Turn. Fold again. A textbook isosceles triangle.

"Did you know," Harvey said, finally breaking his quiet as he tucked the completed triangle into his jacket pocket, "there are over 2,000 varieties of cheese? Mozzarella is the worldwide favorite."

Silence grunted.

They passed a small park, the brick exterior of the adjoining building adorned with a bold cheese-themed mural. A group of tourists posed for photos in front of a giant fiberglass cow painted bold chedar yellow.

The whole scene was almost aggressively wholesome.

Harvey was distracted again, though. He was already folding another receipt.

It was like every other big-chain gas station in America. Refrigerated cases lined the back wall, humming—sodas, diet sodas, and beer. A rack of cheap sunglasses stood near the register, next to impulse-buy lighters and off-brand painkiller-s.Fluorescent lights.

The clerk looked maybe twenty-one, twenty-two. Bored. Chomping gum like it was the only thing keeping her conscious. She wore a shirt a size or two too small, fabric pulled tight across her ample chest, the well-known company logo stretched to the point it was almost unrecognizable. Her nametag said *STEF*.

"Oh, you mean the old broad?" Stef said, still not glancing up. "Yeah, she's been in here every morning this week. Real prim-'n-proper type. Like an old-fashioned librarian but less..." She twirled a finger, summoning the right word. "Less stuffy, ya know. She wore designer glasses, I'll put it that way."

Then, finally, the young woman looked up. Really looked at Silence. It was the first time she had done so, even after flinching at the ruined rasp of his voice when he'd first spoken. Now, her gaze locked onto Silence. Something shifted. A flicker of curiosity. A glint in her eye.

Ugh.

He was at least fifteen years older. Probably more.

For a moment, he half-expected his mind's phantom version of C.C. to throw a sarcastically jealous remark into his thoughts. She often did.

This time, she did not.

"You look a lot like that actor," Stef said, narrowing her eyes and grinning, "What's his name? He was in... um..." A long, lip-chewing pause. "*Cry Baby*! That's what the movie was called."

"Johnny Depp."

"That's the guy! Anyone ever told you that you look like him?"

"Yes."

He got that a lot. The years-earlier incident that left him with a ruined voice had also nearly taken his life, leaving him with a mangled face. The Watchers Specialist plastic surgeon who gave him a new visage did so with an almost artistic flair, taking a lot of creative liberty.

The result visage was angular and brooding, all sharp lines and shadowed hollows, the kind of face people noticed, even when he didn't want them to. He really did look a lot like Johnny Depp.

Only much, much larger.

He realized he hadn't heard from Harvey for a few moments. Turned.

There he was.

Harvey was drifting through the aisles, straightening snack cakes that were already straight, aligning bags of chips. His fingers twitched over a row of gum packs, paused, then nudged one half an inch to the left. His flyway hair sparkled in the sunlight pouring in through the gas station's windows.

Silence turned back to Stef. She smiled, gave her gum a few more strong, deliberate chomps.

"The older woman," he said, swallowed. "She ask any..." Another swallow. "Unusual questions?"

Stef tapped a fingernail against the register, thinking. "Actually, yeah. She asked about some dude who died recently. Some kind of accident." She tilted her head. "It was a little weird, her being from out of town and all."

"She mention..." Silence said, swallowed. "Where she's staying?"

Stef pointed out the window. "Right there."

Silence followed the polished red fingernail and saw it—a big chain hotel, one of the nicer ones. Like the gas station, it sat right off the highway, Wisconsin-23. It was clean and corporate, the sort of place that was just upscale enough to make people feel like they were staying somewhere special. New, too. The lot was lined with young trees, still scrawny, held upright by guy wires.

Stef shrugged. "Seems about right for her. Kinda fancy."

Silence nodded his thanks, paid for the gas, and turned to collect Harvey, who had moved on to the candy bars.

"Almost done," Harvey said without looking up. "Just need to fix the Snickers display. The ratio is all wrong. Did you know color theory in retail spaces can affect purchasing patterns by up to—"

Silence grabbed his arm.

Outside, the Wisconsin summer air hung thick and sweet—it felt alive, pure, tasted good in the nostrils. Harvey practically bounced to the Cadillac, his obsessive rearranging of the gas station's shelves already forgotten, like it had never mattered in the first place.

"That was incredible, Rex!" Harvey said, a massive grin on his face. "Real detective work. The way you questioned her, so subtly, and still got all that info from her—magic! I can't believe how easy you made it look."

Silence slid behind the wheel, ignored the praise. His mind was already mapping out the next move—the hotel.

"I felt like I was in a detective show!" Harvey said and hummed a few notes of one such show's famous theme song. "The way you got her talking, the way you picked up on the smallest details. I'm a pretty detail-oriented person myself!"

No shit.

As they pulled away from the gas station, Silence caught a

glimpse of Harvey's hands already at work. Fold. Crease. Turn. Another triangle was taking shape.

Silence wondered if every last receipt got the same treatment, folded down to a precise little shape before being tucked away like classified intel. A compulsion, clearly. A need for order, for control.

But it was the lesser evil. The real problem was Harvey's talking. The guy filled every moment of quiet, every chance for a bit of peace, with words. He narrated his thoughts, dissected everything around him, spun off into side tangents like a man terrified of nothingness.

Silence could deal with the receipt-folding. But the constant chatter wore thin fast.

He turned the Cadillac onto Wi-23, and the hotel was dead ahead, less than a quarter mile away. Five stories. Clean lines, corporate branding. That row of scrappy lil trees, held up by guy wires, not ready to stand on their own. The porte cochère was too big for Plymouth, like it had been airlifted in from somewhere more ostentatious and just dropped there.

Silence pressed harder on the accelerator. The sooner they found Joanne Daley, the sooner he could untangle whatever mess she'd stumbled into. Then he'd be back on his way to California to rid himself of Harvey and Harvey's endless... Harvey-ness.

But as he drew closer to the hotel, a different thought flitted across his mind: a table.

The hotel's lobby area would have tables, certainly in the continental breakfast area if nowhere else.

And Silence was going to need a table soon. Because he had a letter to write. In less than twenty-four hours.

The first of three letters he'd been instructed to scribe.

The thought made him grimace. Doc Hazel's assignment loomed over him like a dental appointment. Three letters. One to someone he'd wronged. One to someone who'd wronged him. One to someone whose life he'd impacted in an unexpected way.

Who the hell was he supposed to write to?

Someone he'd wronged? In his line of work, most of them were dead.

Someone who'd wronged him? That list was too long to bother sorting through.

"Hey, Rex?" Harvey's voice cut through his thoughts. "Do you think *I'd* be a good detective? Details are important in detective work, right? I really do love detail work. I could be a detective, don't ya think? Huh? Hey. Do ya think?"

Silence flipped on the turn signal.

CHAPTER SEVEN

Too old.

The guy had thought Joanne was too old.

Some nerve that young man had!

She stomped out of the afternoon sunlight and into the artificial chill of the hotel's entrance. The automatic doors whispered shut behind her as she crossed the glassed-in space between the outer and inner doors. She continued through a second set of doors into the lobby.

Too old for this. That's what the desk sergeant had said. Not in so many words, but in that tone, the tone people took with the elderly. The one that made her feel like some dotty grandmother who had wandered off course. She had taught kindergarten for thirty years; she knew condescension when she heard it.

Worse, this rejection she'd just received at the police station meant she'd hit another dead end.

Her hand went to her purse, and her fingers brushed the edge of Layne's envelope. Over the last several days, her deceased former student's letter had become a source of comfort during a continually frustrating situation.

But the letter also served as an accusation. Because Joanne wasn't supposed to be here in Wisconsin.

Tracy was.

But Tracy...

...Tracy was a lost cause.

Another source of comfort lay just behind Layne's letter inside her purse—the small leather-bound journal. Joanne took her fingers off the envelope—and its accusations—and ran them over the journal's smooth leather cover before snapping her purse shut.

The hotel was an upscale chain, its lobby modern and polished, gleaming in the copious sunlight pouring in through all that glass. The check-in desk stretched across the back wall. To one side, a sleek bar and restaurant, empty at this hour, waiting for the evening crowd. On the other side, the breakfast area sat dormant, the counters mostly empty, save for a few remnants of the morning's service.

That was where she saw them.

The man sitting alone at one of the tables was impossible to miss. Large. Brooding. Dark short-sleeve button-up, dark pants, jacket folded over his knee, dress shoes crossed at the ankles, his long legs stretched out to the side. He wasn't eating, wasn't drinking. Just sitting there, motionless, watching the room.

Behind him, a smaller man—with a shock of wild hair, wearing an oversized coat and droopy pants—drifted about the breakfast area, fiddling with whatever was left out. A coffee carafe. A basket of pre-packaged muffins. A stack of napkins. Breakfast had long since ended—it was late afternoon—but the man seemed determined to impose some kind of order on what remained.

Joanne barely had time to process any of it before the big man stood.

And kept standing.

He was even taller than she'd thought, with shoulders that could block out the sun. He took a step.

...toward Joanne.

Then, the other man abandoned his muffin-straightening efforts and followed.

Joanne didn't know what was stranger—that the large man was crossing the lobby toward her or that the small man was evidently his companion. The two of them didn't seem like they belonged together. Not at all. But here they were, walking straight for her.

Joanne stiffened as the big one reached into his pocket.

A ridiculous pulse of apprehension shot through Joanne. What, did she think the guy was about to pull a gun?

All he produced was a wallet from which he retrieved a plastic card. He held it out for Joanne to take.

A moment of hesitation, then she took the card, adjusted her glasses and examined. At first, she thought it was one of the hotel's swipe cards; it was plastic with the correct shape and proportions.

But as she turned it over, she found no magstripe on the back. The plastic was opaque; she could see her palm through it. A pair of dark blue stripes cut diagonally down the left side. Blue, raised lettering gave a message:

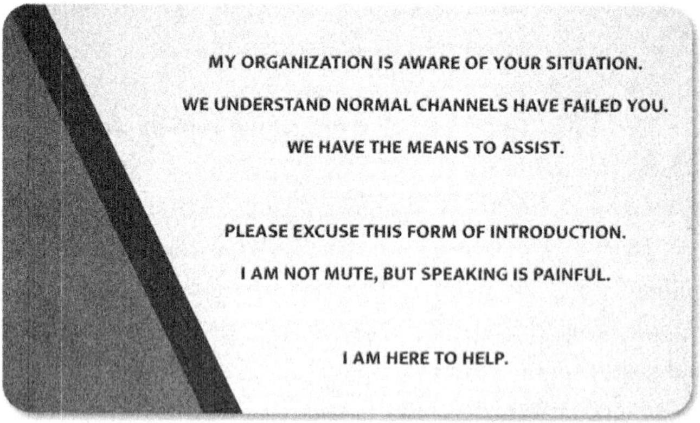
MY ORGANIZATION IS AWARE OF YOUR SITUATION.
WE UNDERSTAND NORMAL CHANNELS HAVE FAILED YOU.
WE HAVE THE MEANS TO ASSIST.
PLEASE EXCUSE THIS FORM OF INTRODUCTION.
I AM NOT MUTE, BUT SPEAKING IS PAINFUL.
I AM HERE TO HELP.

She looked up. "Your 'organization'? What organization?"

No reply.

Odd.

"Are you... a fed or something?" she said.

Again, no reply.

Okay, I'll take that as a yes.

"Who are you?"

"Clay."

Joanne jolted, sucked in a sharp breath.

That voice!

A ruinous, crackling rasp. Harsh and grating, like every word had to claw its way out. Rough. Unnatural. She'd never encountered anything like it.

The other man seemed as shocked as Joanne but for an entirely different reason.

"Rex!" the smaller man blurted in an affronted tone, eyes going wide with bewilderment and hurt. "You're name is Rex! I ... I thought—"

Clay shot his companion a look that immediately shut him up.

The exchange was so sudden and effective that it gave Joanne a chill.

Clay was one imposing son of a bitch.

"Ma'am," Clay said, turning back to her, his voice scraping like sandpaper. He swallowed. "While in Plymouth..." Another swallow. "My name is Clay."

"Just Clay?"

"Just Clay."

Joanne glanced down at the card again. A secretive organization. A man using a one-name alias. It was like something out of a spy novel.

Clay held out his hand.

Joanne placed the card in his palm and said, "So this... organization of yours knows what I'm doing here?"

Clay nodded, returning the card to his wallet.

"But how?"

"We have ways." He swallowed again. "I can help."

The guy swallowed a lot. Whatever was wrong with his throat, it must've hurt like hell.

Joanne studied him, then shifted her gaze to the smaller man, who was now a few feet away, carefully aligning salt and pepper shakers with a table's edge.

"And who's this?"

The man brightened instantly. "Harvey King! Did you know that your name, Joanne, is derived from the Hebrew name Yôḥānāh, meaning 'God is gracious'? It traveled through Greek as Iōánna and Latin as Joanna before becoming Joanne in English and French. Fascinating, isn't it?"

Joanne's lips parted.

Clay shot his companion another look—not as severe this time, more of a look of annoyance.

Joanne fought back a smile despite the situation. They were an odd pair—the towering man of few words and his chattering little shadow.

Then... she hesitated.

If she showed Clay the letter, she was letting him in. Fully. No turning back.

But she'd hit nothing but dead ends in Plymouth. She needed help. She was in over her head—despite Stuart Caruso's support—and there was no more denying that.

Besides, why would someone go through the trouble of printing a plastic business card, tracking her down, and faking a voice like that—like every word had been dragged over broken glass—just to lie to her?

She opened her purse, took out the envelope. "I received this about a week ago. It's what brought me here. Though it wasn't meant for me, not really. It was meant for my daughter, Tracy." She glanced down, ran thumb along the envelope's edge. "Layne was one of my kindergarten students, years ago. Decades. In his letter, he mentions something about shipping manifests and cheese."

Clay shifted. Just a tiny movement, but enough to make her pause. She glanced at him. He held her gaze for a beat, then gave a slight nod that said, *Keep going.*

Joanne had already figured out that Clay was good with nonverbals. Made sense, given his throat. A man who didn't talk much had to learn other communication methods.

"I've hit a few dead ends," she said. "Apparently, I'm not much of a detective. But I do have one more solid lead to check out—Sammy Rud's artisanal cheese shop."

Clay nodded. "We go there."

No debate. No hesitation.

And just like that, Joanne's one-woman effort had just become a team operation.

Harvey bounced on his toes. "Oh! A cheese shop! Did you know that traditional cheese aging techniques involve complex biochemical processes that—" He stopped suddenly, his attention snagged by something over her shoulder. "They have a vending machine!" He looked at Clay. "Do you think it has peanut butter cups? I'm sure it does. *Hope* it does. Speaking of peanut butter cups, did you know the optimal arrangement for a dessert display actually follows the Fibonacci sequence? Loosely, anyway. I'll show you!"

He bounded off, heading for the vending machine in the hallway past the welcome desk, already pulling what appeared to be a small ruler from his pocket.

Clay closed his eyes briefly, then opened them with what looked like immense effort. He gave an *Excuse me* bow to Joanne then trudged toward the hallway.

She watched him follow.

On her own, Joanne's efforts in Plymouth had ground to a halt. That much was clear. But now, this strange pair had appeared out of nowhere, offering help.

Clay approached the vending machine while Harvey enthusiastically demonstrated something with a packet of peanut butter cups and a handful of change.

Strange pair indeed.

But they were there to help.

At this point, what choice did Joanne have but to accept it?

CHAPTER EIGHT

SILENCE PULLED the Cadillac to a stop in front of Rud's Artisanal Cheese Shop.

The place had a quiet, old-world charm. Brick facade. Large windows, slightly fogged with condensation; shelves stacked with cheese wheels visible through the glass. The wooden sign above the door looked hand-carved—the kind of craftsmanship that took time and patience, the same kind of patience Rud probably put into his cheeses.

Silence took it all in, then held a hand toward Joanne in the passenger seat and said, "Letter."

He could have said *May I see the letter from Layne Grosicki?* But he'd purposefully omitted several words.

Much like his frequent swallowing, utilizing broken and abbreviated English was a technique Silence used to help with the torment in his painful throat.

Joanne just looked at him for a moment, confused, then quickly took his meaning. She reached into her purse and pulled out the letter. She unfolded it carefully, smoothing the creases before passing it over.

Silence read.

Dear Mrs. Daley,

It might be strange, after all this time, to receive this letter. You might remember me—Layne Grosicki, kindergarten student, 30 years ago. I've carried pieces of that classroom with me my whole life, for better or worse, and I need your help now in a way I never thought I would.

I want to start by saying I've come to understand that people are complicated. You were, and maybe still are, a complicated person. The way you made me wear that "Speak Clearly" headband hurt me deeply. For years, I hated you for it.

But here's the thing: I've come to realize that your harshness shaped me, too. It made me tougher, more resilient.

I live in Wisconsin now, working as an accountant. I've stumbled onto something: discrepancies in cheese-shipping manifests that I think are tied to something nefarious.

I tried to go through the proper channels, but no one will listen. I have one more lead, a rock-solid one, but I can't trust anyone—except Tracy. I haven't seen her in years, and I couldn't track her down. I assume she must have gotten married and changed her last name...?

That's why I'm writing to you. I need you to pass this letter on to her. She'll know what to do. There's a hidden message in this letter, written in a code only she will understand. It's the only way I can be sure it won't fall into the wrong hands.

Mrs. Daley, I may have hated you for years, but I believe in second chances. Tracy is the only person I can trust, and I'm trusting you to help me reach her.

Sincerely,
Layne Grosicki

Silence read the letter twice.

It wasn't what he expected.

It was raw. Personal. Filled with old wounds and grudges that had lingered for decades. Grosicki had reached out for help, but he hadn't been able to do it without first unloading some old baggage.

The "Speak Clearly" headband... That detail stuck. What the hell was that all about? Whatever it was, it seemed to have scarred Layne. For years. He even told Joanne he'd hated her for it.

Silence turned to Joanne.

She was already looking at him. Their eyes locked, just for a second. She must have sensed what he was thinking because her face changed—her expression tightened, then fell. A flicker of something close to shame. She looked away. Almost mortified.

Silence looked to the back seat. Harvey sat frozen, his always-wide eyes now even wider—secondhand anxiety written all over his face. He hadn't read the letter, but he'd picked up on the tension in the car.

Harvey had an instinct for emotions, reading a room better than most. One of his better traits.

C.C. would have said Harvey was "empathic." She would have liked that about him. She had always told Silence he was the same way—empathic. She admired people who were.

In fact, thinking about it now, Silence figured C.C. would have liked Harvey overall.

Shudder.

Silence considered what Doc Hazel had said earlier that day on the phone when she'd outlined his alternative counseling—his letter-writing assignment. She'd told Silence to consider how one's actions have long-lasting and often unexpected effects on others.

She'd said, *Like ripples in a pond, spreading outward, touching distant shores we never see.*

Silence had thought the idea was preposterous. Holding someone accountable for every little thing? For minor slights, forgotten mistakes, things barely worth remembering? People did things. People moved on. That was how the world worked.

But then there was the woman sitting beside him.

She'd been entrusted with five- and six-year-olds. Shaping them. Molding them. And clearly, some of her actions had lingered. Not for weeks. Not for years.

For decades.

As evidenced by the letter resting in Silence's hands.

To break the awkward quiet, Silence turned back to Joanne and said, "If Layne was looking..." He swallowed. "For your daughter..." Another swallow. "Why here?"

Joanne faced him, still looking shaken. "You mean, why am I, not Tracy, in Wisconsin trying to figure out what happened to Layne?"

Silence nodded.

"Tracy and I have been estranged for years. Many years." Her voice was quieter now. "She's unlisted. I... don't know exactly where she is. Only that she moved to Seattle a long time ago."

Joanne looked away again. A deeper kind of embarrassment this time.

Silence considered this momentarily, then said, "My organization..." He swallowed. "Can find her."

Joanne's head snapped back. "That's impossible."

"No." Silence's voice was calm. Certain.

She just stared at him.

Silence tapped a finger on the letter. "Code?"

Joanne glanced at Layne's print. "Layne and Tracy were good friends when they were little. Both smart kids. Delightfully nerdy. They came up with code games for each other. Anagrams, riddles, stuff like that. Embedded in notes. A language just for the two of them." She shook her head slightly. "It was their thing."

Silence nodded, took that in.

Joanne leaned in. "See this?"

She pointed to several letters, subtly underlined.

Silence nodded. "Noticed that."

Years earlier, when Silence had first joined the Watchers, his training had been intense and thorough. Among the curriculum was the notion of observation. Details mattered. Inconsistencies, even more. No shift too small. No discrepancy too subtle. They drilled it into him, over and over, until his mind worked like a machine.

So he had immediately picked up on the six letters in Layne's message that were subtly, almost imperceptibly, underlined.

T, R, A, R, I, N.

He reached into his pocket, took out his NedNotes brand PenPal notebook, and jotted the letters down.

PenPals were compact but thick, with plastic covers in various bold colors. This one featured green and yellow chevron stripes.

Before the Watchers—before the ruined throat, before the new identity—Silence's previous incarnation, Jake Rowe, had used notebooks to organize his thoughts. Now, the habit remained, and sometimes, he used the pages to write messages for others when his abbreviated English tactics wouldn't suffice.

He stared at the letters he'd just written down. *T, R, A, R, I, N.* Tried to make sense of them.

Joanne frowned. "Is it an anagram?"

Harvey, in the back seat, leaned forward. "Could be. Or maybe a riddle? Or some kind of sequence? You know, cryptography has been used in messages for centuries. Some of the earliest known ciphers date back to the—"

"Harvey," Silence said.

Harvey stopped.

Joanne exhaled. "I don't see the pattern."

Silence didn't either. Not yet.

Another dead end. For now.

Silence snapped the PenPal shut and returned it to his pocket. He handed the letter back to Joanne. Then he opened the door.

Time to move.

Joanne followed. Harvey climbed out behind her.

A few moments later, they pushed through the wooden door and stepped inside Rud's Artisanal Cheese Shop.

The place was warm and inviting. A medley of rich aromas hit them—cheddar, gouda, brie. The polished wooden floors gleamed. Display cases filled with cheese occupied the center, while shelves lining the walls boasted crackers, jams, and other accompaniments. A half dozen or so workers milled around a similar number of customers.

A happenin' little place.

Joanne took a step ahead of Silence, leading them toward a man at the far end of the shop, arranging a display of cheese wedges. He turned as they approached, a friendly smile breaking across his face.

This must be Sammy Rud.

Black. Mid-fifties. Average height. Round and more than a little plump, but it suited him—it matched his easy, welcoming presence. His dark skin contrasted with his bright white apron, worn over a light blue dress shirt.

"Mr. Rud, hello," Joanne said. "I'm Joanne Daley. We spoke on the phone."

Rud smiled warmer. "Yes, of course. You were asking

about... the fella who died in town a week or so ago, right? The guy from Milwaukee?"

"That's right."

Rud's gaze shifted to Silence, his expression staying warm but growing curious. "And who are your friends?"

Joanne hesitated just a second. "This is ... Clay. He's a ... private investigator."

Silence rolled with it.

During his missions—particularly while conducting the investigative components—Silence was often assumed to have one of three professions: federal agent, police officer, or private detective. Often, he let these assumptions fly for the sake of simplicity and prudence.

Joanne turned. "And this is Clay's, um, assistant. Harvey."

Harvey beamed but remained mercifully quiet.

Rud's gaze lingered on Silence for a beat, then he nodded and turned back to Joanne.

"Did you know Layne personally?" he asked Joanne, his voice softer now.

Joanne hesitated. "Yes... sort of... a long time ago."

Rud sighed. "Sorry for your loss."

Joanne gave a slight nod of appreciation, though she looked flustered by the exchange, ready to move forward with the conversation.

"Layne came by not long before his accident," Rud continued. "Was asking about shipping manifests. Said he'd found an alarming discrepancy." He shook his head. "I couldn't tell him much. I own the business, sure, but I'm not much of a businessman. Just a cheese man." He gave a small, self-deprecating chuckle. "I let my business manager handle the paperwork."

"Who's that?" Silence said.

Rud went wide-eyed and stared at Silence for a moment—a standard first-timer reaction to Silence's awful voice.

A moment passed, then Rud gulped and said, "Margaret Sloan. Sharp as they come. Runs the books, keeps the place running smooth." He poked a wedge of cheese back into alignment with the others. "I told Layne I'd check in with her, see if she could make sense of what he found. But by the time I did..." He trailed off.

"Layne was already dead," Joanne said quietly.

Rud nodded.

"What did..." Silence said, swallowed. "Margaret find?"

Rud shrugged. "Nothing. Sorry, but she found nothing out of the ordinary."

Joanne turned to Silence. Crestfallen.

Silence read her expression: *Another dead end.*

But then Rud spoke again.

"Listen... if you're looking into something bad in this town, I'll tell you this much—Wayne Durante's the guy you want to look at."

Silence said, "Durante?"

Rud nodded. "Of the little crime we have around Plymouth, most of it goes through him. He runs a pool hall in town—Kick Shot. Supposedly just a place to rack 'em up, have a drink. But there's always been rumors..."

"Such as?" Silence said.

Rud exhaled. "Depends on who you ask. Some say Durante runs illegal card games—high-stakes poker, off-the-books sports betting. Others think he moves stolen goods through there—power tools, farm equipment, anything that can turn a quick profit. And then there are the rumors about drugs. Pills, mostly. Some say fentanyl."

"The cops?" Silence said.

Rud gave a dry chuckle. "Durante's careful. He keeps the front business clean, and nothing ever seems to stick. People whisper, but no one talks too loud."

Silence took that in.

Wayne Durante. A new name, a new thread to pull.

Joanne turned to him. There was a shift in her posture now, a spark of purpose reignited behind her aging eyes.

This wasn't a dead end after all.

"Now, if you'll excuse me," Rud said, smile returning, "I have a batch of havarti curds that isn't gonna stir itself."

CHAPTER NINE

The smell was pungent.

Fresh blacktop.

Joanne walked alongside Clay and Harvey on the sidewalk skirting the brand-new parking lot—jet black, glaring white lines.

Ahead was their objective, a massive office building. Three stories of blue glass, sleek and modern. Steel and reflective surfaces. Built to impress. It looked like it had been plucked from a corporate hub and dropped here, entirely out of place in Plymouth.

Which, most likely, was the point.

Set far on the edge of town—off Wisconsin-23—it felt like a statement. Deliberate. Separated from the quaint downtown.

A sleek fountain sat just before it, water bubbling over stacked stone—a forced attempt at elegance but an effective one.

Beyond the fountain, fields stretched wide, bright green under a bold blue sky with trees lining the distance. But some of that open land wouldn't stay open for long. The groundwork was there—cleared lots, the faint outlines of future roads. The first steps toward more buildings, more pavement, more expansion.

Joanne nodded toward the building as they walked. "From what I understand, the city partially subsidized this place, hoping it would kickstart a whole business park out here." She glanced at the developing landscape. "Looks like it's working."

Clay took it in, silent as ever.

Harvey, trailing a step behind, sniffed dramatically. "You smell that? That's new blacktop. You know, fresh asphalt contains volatile organic compounds, VOCs, that are released into the air during curing. Not exactly great for air quality."

Clay didn't respond. Joanne didn't either.

Harvey cleared his throat, unfazed. "They got a nice fountain, though! You like it, Clay?"

A moment earlier, Joanne had caught Clay staring at the fountain as they walked.

Something flickered behind his dark eyes—a thought, a memory, something. For just a second, he looked almost unguarded, almost vulnerable.

Joanne had seen that look before. In her classroom. On five-year-olds staring out the window, lost in thoughts too big for them to explain.

Seeing the expression on someone like Clay—large, severe, and possibly violent—was startling. But also, in an odd way, charming.

All the same, Clay's response to Harvey's question—whether he liked the fountain—was nothing but a curt grunt.

Joanne let the moment pass, then spoke. "Stuart Caruso has been the only friendly face in Plymouth since I got here."

Clay turned his head slightly, listening.

"He's the only person who's even given a shred of credibility to the idea that Layne was murdered," Joanne continued. "Everyone else either dismisses me outright or acts like I'm some grieving old woman seeing ghosts."

Harvey, still lagging behind, jogged up to them. "Why? What's Caruso's deal?"

"He came in from Milwaukee. Like Layne did," Joanne said. "He's a food inspector—been in town following up on what Layne found in those shipping manifests." She shook her head. "Layne unearthed something bad. Caruso was the only one who thought it was worth looking into."

Clay absorbed that. Didn't respond. But Joanne could tell —he was filing it away.

The automatic doors hissed open, and they stepped into the sterile, modern lobby.

Polished concrete, floor-to-ceiling glass. Large televisions mounted on the walls cycled through stock footage of happy people doing happy things. Smaller screens showed local event photos. In the center of the space, a circle of orange leather chairs. In the back, a bank of elevators.

Harvey let out a low whistle. "Corporate minimalism at its finest. Modernism mixed with just a dash of existential dread."

Joanne ignored him and led the way down a back hallway. The smooth finishes and high-end fixtures remained the same...

...until the effect faltered.

The offices tucked away in the back were different. Less polish, fewer frills. Lower-rent space, shoved out of sight.

Stuart Caruso's office was one of them.

The door was open, and the office inside was small and cramped, a contrast to the building's grandeur.

No windows. No space beyond the essentials. Just a basic desk, a landline phone, and paperwork—everywhere. Stacks covered the desk, peeked out from an overloaded filing cabinet, littered a side table.

Caruso sat behind the desk, flipping through a file. He glanced up, registered Joanne, then stood to greet them.

"Ms. Daley. A pleasure to see you again." He'd said it cordially enough, but it was clear her visit wasn't an unexpected pleasure—he looked busy. "You brought friends this time."

"This is Clay," Joanne said. Then, remembering the earlier lie, "He's a private investigator."

Caruso's eyes flicked to Clay. A moment stretched between them. Not hostile, not welcoming. Just... reading.

Harvey didn't wait for an introduction. "And I'm Harvey King. Assistant to the PI. Researcher. Data analyst. General facilitator of fact-finding." He grinned. "Think of me as the Watson to his Holmes."

Caruso's expression shifted, something between curiosity and amusement. His eyes lingered on Harvey for half a second, then turned back to Clay.

"A private investigator?" he repeated. "I assume you're here to help Joanne with the Layne Grosicki matter?"

Clay nodded.

Caruso sighed, rubbing the back of his neck. "Joanne, I get it. You want answers. I do, too. But I came to Plymouth on a limb. My boss barely signed off on it. I don't want to make the case look sloppy by letting too many hands get involved." He gestured at the stacks of paperwork in front of him. "I worked hard just to get here to this tiny little office. If I step wrong, they'll pull me back before I can finish the job. And Grosciki died for this." He paused. "Whether he died by accident or... by some other means, like you seem to think, I owe it to him to figure this thing out. The *right* way."

Clay took a step forward.

"Just want..." he said and swallowed. "Information."

Caruso tilted his head slightly, taking in the calamity that was Clay's voice. A moment passed, then, "Let me guess—you want to see the data and notes Grosicki passed on to me?"

Clay said nothing. Just waited.

Caruso exhaled, his jaw working like he was chewing over a decision. Then he shook his head.

"I'm not handing over everything." He hesitated, then added, "But I can tell you this much: Grosicki was convinced multiple cheese vendors across Plymouth had simultaneously shipped tainted product. He dug into the shipping manifests, crunched the data, and found something that scared him."

Joanne and Clay exchanged a glance.

Harvey tapped a finger against his chin. "Statistically, simultaneous contamination across multiple vendors without a common distributor is unlikely. That suggests either coordinated sabotage or a failure in oversight."

Caruso looked at him. "Uh-huh..."

"Any businesses..." Clay said, swallowed. "In particular?"

Caruso studied them for a moment, then exhaled. "Layne mentioned Rud's Cheese Shop more than once."

"We were just there," Joanne said.

Caruso smirked faintly. "Yeah, I checked up on Rud's shop myself. The port authority records show one denied shipment a month ago. Hardly a conspiracy. Rud's clean. But Layne was also looking at Wayne Durante. Now *that* guy is where you folks need to be looking if you really think Grosicki was murdered."

Clay said, "Rud pointed us..." He swallowed. "That way too."

Caruso nodded. Looked at Clay for a moment. Rubbed the back of his neck again. Then, abruptly, he turned, pulled open a desk drawer, and took out a dog-eared, beer-stained slip of paper. He tossed it across the desk.

Clay pinned it with a finger, picked it up.

Joanne leaned over, took a look.

The paper was creased, stained, and cheaply printed, like it had been run off an inkjet with a fading cartridge. Kick Shot's logo was slapped at the top—a scuffed-up eight-ball with a cracked cue stick behind it.

EXCLUSIVE TOURNAMENT NIGHT – INVITE ONLY
Friday – 8 PM
Kick Shot – Plymouth, WI
NO ENTRY WITHOUT THIS PASS

Below that, a scrawled signature—probably Durante's—more a lazy squiggle than a name.

"Here. A literal ticket inside," Caruso said. "Durante's hosting a high-stakes pool tournament tonight. Invitation-only. Even for spectators. Kick Shot's shutting down to the public for the night—just players, guests, and whoever Durante wants inside."

Harvey stepped closer, looked at the card, and grimaced. "*Bleh*. Real classy place."

Clay pocketed the invite and told Caruso, "Thanks."

CHAPTER TEN

As much as McCrorie hated the abandoned dairy factory, there was no denying its efficacy. It had proven itself the perfect base of operations in Plymouth.

Certain activities were just easier in a zone of rusted-out decay than in the polished, civilized world. One such activity was murder—the recent execution of Tom Weiler.

But there were other dark activities than killing that required a theatrically deft touch.

Like intimidation.

Sure, McCrorie could have grabbed Sammy Rud in the man's sissy cheese shop. Dragged him into the back storage room, maybe out into the alley.

There were plenty of ways for McCrorie to throw his weight around, to make Rud sweat.

But the old factory was the most effective option.

The place sat on a forgotten edge of Plymouth—far from the quaint downtown and its charming storefronts like Rud's. The skeletal steel remains climbed into the brightening morning sky—jagged and broken. Rusted milk tanks streaked with sediment. Cracked concrete floor. Scattered pallets and plastic crates.

Forgotten and dead.

And intimidating.

Especially with the noises coming from the man hidden far in the depths of the facility. The man wasn't banging on the walls this time. He was screaming.

Sounded like a damn ghost.

Which made Rud shake all the more.

A few yards before him, Sammy Rud's round figure was small against the vast backdrop of decay. McCrorie watched the older man, a predator assessing his prey.

"An older woman?" McCrorie said.

Rud nodded. Too quickly. His entire figure was quaking. "Yes. Her name was Joanne. Joanne Daley."

"And the men with her?"

"One guy was... I don't know, like a vagrant or something. Frizzy hair, oversized jacket, wild eyes. The other guy was..." he trailed off.

"Was what?"

"A private detective."

"*What?*"

Rud just nodded, shaking harder, avoiding McCrorie's glare.

"I saw your security footage," McCrorie said. "The big guy? You're talking about that huge son of a bitch in the dark clothes? *That's* Joanne Daley's private eye?"

Rud nodded again, shaking harder. He still wouldn't look at McCrorie.

"Shit!" McCrorie said and shoved his hands in his pockets. He stomped a yard away into the debris, spun on his heel, and came back at Rud, who flinched, folding in on himself.

Rud's warm, approachable demeanor now worked against him, amplifying his utter feebleness. He was the kind of man built for chatting with customers about Gorgonzola, not standing in the ruins of a dead factory, answering questions from men like McCrorie. His dark eyes darted around like he was searching for an exit. But there was none.

Pathetic.

"They... they were asking about Layne Grosicki," Rud stammered, words tumbling out in a rush. "You know, that guy who died last week."

"Yes, I'm aware..." McCrorie muttered on a growl.

"The private detective, Clay. He didn't say much. And he had this crazy voice. I mean, it didn't even sound human. It was so crackling and—"

McCrorie's pulse ticked higher.

He snapped.

"Shut up!" His voice ripped through the dead factory, bouncing off steel and concrete. "I don't give a shit about the guy's voice."

Rud jumped, looked away.

"I told you, I saw the security tape," McCrorie continued. "I saw how this Clay moves—his stance, his awareness, the way he carries himself. This guy is no everyday private detective."

McCrorie thought again of the footage he'd studied minutes before his men dragged Rud before him on the crumbling remains of the old factory.

The large man who'd stood behind the older woman—along with the squirrely guy with the flyaway hair—had a certain presence. A weight. A determination Rud had seen before but never in a place like Plymouth.

No, Clay was not a P.I.

He was something else. Something trained. Something dangerous.

Which was a serious problem.

And McCrorie didn't like problems.

The rusted walls were still buzzing with the last shout he proctored upon Rud. The towering milk silos stood still, listening. The rusting pipes dripped water somewhere deep in the nothingness.

Then, lower, McCrorie said, "And you weren't going to tell me?"

Rud nodded fast, bobbing like a fool, desperate for McCrorie's mercy. "No! I was. I just... I just needed time to process it all before I got a hold of you."

McCrorie turned away, jaw tight. Couldn't look at the idiot any longer.

But as he turned, even more disgust twisted inside him. Not at Rud this time. At himself.

Look at the guy. Round, soft, weak. A cheese shop owner, for shit's sake. A man who spent his days talking about gouda and brie, smiling at customers, making small talk about dairy farms.

And McCrorie had been stupid enough to get himself involved with a pussy like this.

What the hell had he been thinking?

He clenched his teeth.

McCrorie exhaled sharply. Pushed Rud from his mind. Focused on what mattered.

Clay.

This guy wasn't just a new player in the game. He was a game-changer, the kind who could flip the board and send the pieces flying.

Shit, McCrorie hated problems...

McCrorie gave Rud one last look, long and hard. Then, he turned away, pulling his cellular phone from his pocket as he walked, flipping it open.

There was an important call to place.

CHAPTER ELEVEN

Back at the hotel.

The business center was tucked just off the lobby, a cramped room with two computers and a printer. It smelled faintly of toner and recycled air. The hum of the fluorescent lighting overhead was just a bit too loud.

Silence sat at one of the computers. He drummed his fingers against the desktop as he stared at the empty inbox on the screen. The Watchers' response on Wayne Durante was inbound. Any second now.

Since the Watchers conducted their illegal and clandestine work by slipping in and out of U.S. government channels, they had access to ahead-of-the-curve technology that wouldn't be revealed to the general public until the twenty-first century. More often than not, this was incredibly helpful to Silence.

Sometimes, however, it was just a tease. Because cutting-edge technology is frequently useless without an accompanying infrastructure. As a Watcher, Silence knew that someday, in the not-so-distant future, the Internet would be wireless and portable.

For now, Silence was tied down by wires like everyone else in the 1990s. This meant that when he was in the field, he spent a lot of time like this sitting on his ass at a computer somewhere, linking himself up to the Watchers' copious illegal backdoor technologies.

A few moments earlier, he'd made a quick call via his cellular phone, holding down the 2 button for a speed dial option. The setting was designed to roulette-spin his call through a network, linking him to a different Specialist each time he used it.

"Specialist," the woman had said.

Silence proceeded with protocol, issuing the standard Asset introduction: code name and number. "Suppressor, A-23."

"Confirmed. State your business."

"Information retrieval," Silence said and swallowed. "Wayne Durante. Plymouth..." Another swallow. "Wisconsin."

"Anything else?"

"Contact info for Tracy..." He swallowed. "Simmons née Daley. Seattle."

Rustling to the side.

Silence had turned to see Joanne adjusting in her chair. Uncomfortable. Fidgeting anxiously with a small leather-bound journal.

"Five minutes," the woman had said.

Beep.

And that was it.

That had been three minutes and seventeen seconds earlier.

One hundred ninety-seven seconds of pure Harvey...

The guy was sitting way too close to Silence in the cramped confines and buzzing with excitement—not about the investigation, not about the intrigue of potential murder, not even about the fact that Silence was electronically skirting past legal channels in a way that should have made an ordinary civilian uneasy.

No, Harvey was fixated on the vending machine find of the century.

"I can't believe they have these!" Harvey exclaimed, holding up a crinkling black-and-gold package of Midnight Branch Licorice. His eyes were wide with joy. "I thought they stopped carrying this brand outside of specialty stores! Oh, man, I've got to see what else they have in this machine before we leave. Try 'em!"

Silence barely looked away from the screen. "No."

"Come on, Clay! Midnight Branch is the best licorice on the market." Harvey shook the bag, grinning like a kid on Christmas. "You've got to try one."

Silence frowned. "I don't eat..." He swallowed. "Black licorice."

Harvey gasped like Silence had just confessed to murder. "That's ridiculous! You're missing out on a complex flavor profile. Bold, deep, sophisticated."

Silence grunted.

Harvey was undeterred. He ripped open the bag and pulled out a single, jet-black twist. "Try it. One piece. You'll thank me later."

Silence shook his head.

"Come *on*," Harvey pressed, wiggling the licorice under Silence's nose. "You survived shootouts, explosions, people trying to kill you. And you're scared of a little licorice?"

Silence glared at him. "Not scared."

"Then eat it."

Silence glared harder.

In his head, C.C. sighed. *Oh, stop being stubborn, love. He's a sweet soul. Just humor him.*

Silence sighed once more, this time out loud. Took the damn licorice. Popped it in his mouth.

And immediately regretted it.

The taste hit him like a punch, a real haymaker. Bitter, herbal, cloying. He chewed once, grimaced, and forced it down.

Harvey beamed. "See? Fantastic, right?"

Silence didn't respond. He wanted to rinse his mouth out with rubbing alcohol.

Across the cramped space, Joanne had been watching all of this. She was leaning against the opposite desktop, arms crossed, smiling.

Not just smiling. Amused.

Maybe even charmed.

Silence felt ridiculous. He could take down an armed attacker in seconds, could disappear into a city without a trace—yet here he was, being force-fed licorice by a man who organized gas station candy by label color.

He could only imagine what Joanne was thinking.

Probably mentally placing this moment over memories of five-year-olds squabbling over snacks in her old kindergarten classroom.

However, for the first few minutes in the business center, before Harvey came bursting back in with his licorice, fresh from his vending machine adventure, Joanne had been writing. Head down, wholly absorbed in her journal.

It had felt wrong to Silence.

Given the gravity of the situation—trying to figure out how her former student died, she should have been more present. More engaged. Instead, she'd been somewhere else, lost in her own thoughts.

Now, after her momentary amusement with Silence and Harvey's interaction, she went right back to the journal, leaning back in her chair. Her head was tilted slightly, her expression thoughtful as she wrote.

Hmm...

Silence reminded himself what Doc Hazel had said—that school records showed numerous parental complaints against Joanne Daley during her years as a kindergarten teacher.

Apparently, she was a mean, unsympathetic bitch, Doc Hazel had said.

This woman had impacted her daughter so profoundly that Tracy had severed all contact for years. She'd left such a mark on Layne Grosicki that, in one of his final acts, he'd felt compelled to call her out in the same letter where he begged for her daughter's help.

Ripples of influence, of destruction, lasting for years.

The ripple effect.

The butterfly effect.

Perhaps it shouldn't have surprised Silence that Joanne was more invested in her journal than the investigation.

Harvey was still rattling on. "I mean, you do like it, right? Huh, Clay?"

Hell no, I don't like it, he thought but didn't say.

Harvey was about to launch into more, but a ping from the computer saved Silence.

Silence immediately turned away from Harvey and clicked open the email. The Watchers' profile on Wayne Durante was finally here.

As well as the contact information for Joanne's daughter, Tracy.

Silence took out his PenPal notebook and quickly jotted down Tracy's info. Then he pocketed it again and settled in to absorb the intel about Durante.

Wayne Durante. Forty-eight years old. Caucasian. Lifelong Plymouth resident. In the digital photos, Durante's appearance perfectly reflected his reputation—a rugged, intimidating build that suggested years of physical confrontations. Hard features. Rough hands. Five o'clock shadow in every one of the photos.

Durante operated a side hustle out of his run-down pool hall—Kick Shot—offering high-interest loans to desperate townspeople and enforcing debts with an iron fist. He supplemented his income through a seemingly legal fishing charter business, which doubled as a front for laundering money. Many locals grudgingly respected him for providing quick cash in tough times, but his methods—intimidation and occasional violence—were heavy-handed.

He was also rumored to dabble in narcotics distribution.

Dabbling by the truckload.

Silence leaned back in his chair, fingers steepled before his face. Wayne Durante was intriguing. Tough exterior with darker layers underneath. But how did he fit into Layne's investigation—one that revolved around cheese shipping manifests?

For now, Silence pushed back from the computer station, stepping away from Mr. Licorice and moving toward Joanne's chair. Her pen moved steadily across the page, her focus unbroken.

Silence tapped her shoulder.

She jumped, startled—completely absorbed in whatever she was writing.

Yes, very odd...

Joanne looked up. "Did you dig up some useful info?"

Silence nodded. "But now, you..." he said and swallowed. "Gotta make the call."

He took his PenPal from his pocket, tore off the sheet with Tracy's phone number, and held it out.

There was a long moment when Joanne just stared at the paper before finally taking it.

CHAPTER TWELVE

Seattle, Washington

If Tracy Simmons wasn't more careful, she was going to ruin the old photograph.

She realized that the corner of the Polaroid was beginning to bend where she was working it between her fingers, massaging out some of the anxiety as she stared out her window.

She stopped herself. She couldn't damage the photo. It was too precious for that. Too old. Too important. Sacred, even.

She was on the couch, one leg curled beneath her, the other foot pressed into the woven fabric of the well-worn rug — the one that had traveled with her from apartment to apartment, city to city within the Seattle metro area. Hardwood floors stretched beyond it, leading to her small kitchen, her office nook, and the single bedroom that made up the rest of her world.

She had built this place herself. A modest apartment, nothing flashy, nothing anyone would show off in a magazine.

But it was hers. Every inch of it. She'd filled it with earthy tones, mismatched but intentional. A well-loved couch draped with a faded throw. Shelves lined with dog-eared books, vintage cameras, and souvenirs from places she'd shot assignments. The walls were covered in art—some framed, some pinned up, a mix of her own photographs and pieces she'd collected from local artists.

No, it wasn't much. And plenty of people might have turned their noses up to it. But Tracy had worked hard for this place, carved it out on a freelance photographer's income in a city that wasn't cheap.

She'd done it without her mother.

Despite her mother.

And now, her mother's voice sat in that box on the table.

A little piece of Joanne Daley, right there in her home. Uninvited. Invading.

Tracy stared at the answering machine. The red LCD screen burned into her vision, the phone number it displayed, particularly those first three digits—the area code.

805.

A California area code. Most of Ventura, Santa Barbara, and San Luis Obispo counties.

Morro Bay...

Tracy's past. Her mother.

She had ignored the call. But the message had come anyway.

The first time she'd listened, she hadn't truly processed it —she'd been unable to get past the shock of hearing Mom's voice in her sacred space. She had listened again, forcing herself to absorb the words.

And now, she leaned forward, stabbed a finger into the PLAY button for a third listen.

The machine clicked, then, "Hey, Tracy. It's... well, it's Mom. Uh, good morning."

Tracy's jaw clenched.

"I know this is out of nowhere, and I'm so sorry for invading your privacy. But I want you to know—I didn't do anything sneaky or nefarious to find your number. I wouldn't be reaching out if it wasn't important."

A pause. Tracy could hear her mother breathing.

"Listen, Layne Grosicki—you know, from school?—he sent me a letter. He wanted me to find you. He said you were the only person who could help him."

Tracy's grip on the photo tightened.

"He was investigating something here in Wisconsin, something he thought was dangerous. And... honey, I'm sorry to tell you this, but Layne is dead."

There it was again. Said out loud. It made it more real.

Tracy's stomach turned. Layne. Gone.

She looked at the photograph, which blurred as her eyes grew hot and moist again.

There was Layne. In the golden tones of time-faded photography. Seven years old. Tracy was beside him. Also seven years old. A swing set directly behind them. Beyond that, a parking lot full of now-antique vehicles.

After nearly twenty years of silence between them. After she had assumed Layne had gone on with life, forgotten about her entirely. But no—he had trusted her, even after all this time.

Somehow, inconceivably, Tracy had been the person Layne thought of so many years later when he had been at his most desperate point.

And now, it was too late.

The message droned on.

"I'm here in Plymouth, Wisconsin, now, with... um, Clay, a private investigator. We could really use your help. Layne said you were the only one who could decipher a code he hid in the letter he sent me."

A long pause.

"I would have reached out sooner, when I first got it, before... before Layne died. But I only recently met Clay. He's the one who found you."

Another pause.

"Please, honey, please call me back. It's... it's important. 805-555-6439. That's my cellular. Um... thank you."

A shuffling sound. Then nothing.

Click.

The tape stopped.

Tracy stared at the machine, breathing through her nose, nostrils flaring, chest shaking.

Layne Grosicki was dead.

A tear escaped, streaked down her cheek.

She let out a sharp breath and flipped the Polaroid over again, couldn't look at it any longer.

If Layne was dead, why then was Mom calling her about the letter, claiming to be in Wisconsin playing Sherlock Holmes... with the assistance of a freakin' private detective, no less.

There was only one answer.

Mom was using Layne's death as leverage. Emotional manipulation. A pathetic and cruel attempt to pass off a fresh intrusion in Tracy's life as "necessary."

Despicable.

Unbelievable.

Yet, so like Mom.

So calculated.

Tracy exhaled sharply and set the Polaroid facedown on the table. Her hands itched for one of her cameras, to grip it, to feel its weight, the certainty of knowing she was in control of something.

She flicked her eyes to the window. Seattle's gray sky had

finally cleared. Sunlight cut across the deck, hitting the wooden railing, dappling the floor in patches of warmth.

She'd always loved this view.

Loved the openness—this little patch of quasi-nature she'd found right in the middle of the city, the trees swaying in the distance. It had reminded her of freedom. A clean break from the past.

Now, it seemed, that past had forced its way in despite Tracy's monumental efforts.

Tracy nodded, resolve hardening. She wasn't going to get involved, wasn't going to fly across the country, wasn't going to help.

Let Mom play detective in Wisconsin alone.

Maybe someday that mean old hag would finally realize—some things were gone for good.

CHAPTER THIRTEEN

Plymouth, Wisconsin

THE PINK LIGHT of dusk spilled through the hotel's massive window walls, drenching the lobby. The floors reflected it in streaks of rose and gold, and the deep leather chairs near the windows took on an amber hue.

Even the long expanse of dark wood at the check-in desk gleamed differently under the changing sky.

The clerk squinted against the glare and smiled as Silence and Harvey approached, pulling his attention away from a sleek, new computer. It had one of those new "flat-screen" monitors that had been popping up lately.

As Silence approached, Harvey fell into place behind him, immediately beginning a self-imposed task of reorganizing the tourist brochure rack while simultaneously patting the tiny lump on the front of his jacket—Mitsy, in her place of prominence, the left breast pocket.

"The Wisconsin Dells pamphlets really should go before Waterparks," he muttered, shuffling glossy paper. "And someone has completely disregarded proper alphabetization protocols for the cheese tour offerings."

The clerk glanced over. Then, quickly back to Silence.

"Two rooms," Silence said and swallowed. "Adjacent."

Harvey appeared at his elbow.

"Actually, about room arrangements—I've been analyzing optimal spatial configurations for surveillance scenarios. If we implement a diagonal positioning, then—"

"Two rooms," Silence repeated. "Adjacent."

Harvey huffed but didn't push it. Something caught his attention, and he turned, eyes drifting toward the floor-to-ceiling lobby windows.

Silence followed his gaze.

Across the street, a wiry young man in his early twenties stood in the doorway of Pete's Pawn & Loan, the roughest-looking place in a partially inhabited strip mall. The kid's posture was tense, and he held a beat-up laptop like it was his last lifeline. Sandy-blond hair, unkempt. Gaunt face. Darting eyes. He wore jeans and a faded hoodie that hung loose over his frame.

He was pleading.

Across from him, the Pete's Pawn representative—Pete himself, quite possibly—stood firm, blocking the entrance with his bulk. Thick arms crossed over a bulbous stomach that stretched his stained tank top. Greasy pants, scuffed boots, and the demeanor of a man who didn't take crap from anyone—because he'd been offered so much of it.

The kid held out the laptop, gesturing frantically. Pete shook his head, stabbed a finger toward the parking lot—*Get lost.*

The kid's eyes went wide, desperate. He said something else. Pete snapped back, face twisting, cheeks reddening. He moved forward, forcing the kid to back away from the doorway.

Not a negotiation. A shut-down.

The kid clutched the laptop to his chest, backing up another step.

Pete pointed again, this time more aggressive. A warning.

The kid looked ready to break, ready to bawl his eyes out right there in front of a crummy pawn shop.

"What's going on over there, ya figure, Clay?" Harvey asked, staring, intrigued.

"Nothing," Silence said and swallowed. "Local drama."

Yes, local drama. Silence had assessed it in a second. He seemed subconsciously wired to detect trouble brewing in the everyday corners of life. A radar, always scanning.

His boss at the Watchers, Falcon, had a rule: *No involvement in local matters*.

Silence hated that rule and loved breaking it.

And break it, he did. Frequently.

Which led to a lot of trouble.

In fact, Silence had just broken Falcon's *No involvement in local matters* rule a month earlier.

Driving home to Pensacola, Florida, after completing a mission, he'd stopped at a gas station in Tennessee. He'd needed to pee. He'd wanted a bottle of water and a pack of Wrigley's chewing gum.

Someone else entered as he was checking out, this individual wearing a ski mask and too much confidence. The guy waved a Glock at the cashier—a teenage kid, wide-eyed and stiff as a board.

Silence had moved before he even thought about it.

Instinct. Training. Couldn't turn it off.

Thirty seconds later, the gun was on the floor, the would-be robber was hog-tied with his own shoelaces, and the kid at the register was still standing there, still holding Silence's pack of Wrigley's, looking stunned.

Security footage had almost put Silence's face on the local

news. Only a last-minute electronic interception by Watchers Specialists had stopped that from happening.

Falcon had been... upset.

This had been less than a month earlier.

So now, Silence was walking on eggshells.

As he looked out the window at the pawnshop, he could almost hear Falcon's baritone voice in his head: *No involvement in local matters.*

Silence didn't need to piss off his boss any further.

Besides, nothing truly bad seemed to be happening at the pawn shop—just a desperate man in a desperate situation, trying desperately to claw his way out of it by selling a battered laptop.

Hell, the computer was probably stolen.

Love! C.C.'s voice chided in his mind. *Don't be a presumptuous asshole. You have no idea about that young man's situation.*

She was right. She always was.

Nonetheless, Silence was sure nothing at the pawn shop would require his intervention. No point in pissing off Falcon any more than he already had.

Harvey was sure transfixed, though. His eyes stayed locked on the pawn shop scene, his hands moving automatically—folding a receipt. Crease. Turn. Fold.

The clerk cleared his throat. "Will that be credit?"

"Cash," Silence said, reaching for his wallet.

Paying in cash was a standard Watchers practice. It kept things clean. No footprint.

The clerk took the cash and made change.

Silence held out a palm. "Keep it."

"Thank you, sir," the clerk said, putting the extra bills aside. "And a credit card for incidentals?"

Silence slapped two more hundred-dollar bills on the counter and slid them over.

A moment passed. "Very good, sir."

Gotta love cash. It always did the trick. No footprint.

Silence's attention shifted back to Harvey's compulsive folding. The man's fingers moved frantically, even as his eyes remained glued to the pawnshop argument.

The printer behind the desk spat out a receipt, which the clerk handed to Silence along with a card key. He gave another card key to Harvey. "Rooms 214 and 216. Second floor, take a right—"

Harvey was already folding the card's paper sleeve.

"Harvey!" Silence's voice snapped, cutting off the clerk. "Knock it off!"

The damn folding never ceased—receipts, brochures, key sleeves—like the world would fall apart if a scrap of paper wasn't turned into a triangle.

Shit!

The lobby fell silent.

Harvey flinched, his fingers freezing mid-fold.

The clerk blinked.

And Silence swallowed, pulsing the spot of pain in his throat.

"Sorry," Harvey mumbled. But even as he spoke, his hands were completing the triangle.

Ugh.

Silence pocketed his card key and stalked toward the elevator.

A few moments later, they were inside as the elevator wheezed its way to the second floor.

Harvey stood in the corner. "That kid at the pawn shop, the way his hands were shaking—clear indicators of autonomic stress response. I once read a fascinating paper on the physiological manifestations of financial desperation—"

"Local drama," Silence said and swallowed. "Not our concern."

The elevator doors slid open.

Harvey followed him down the hall, which was clean, air-conditioner-chilly, and smelled of antiseptic spray. "But the micro-expressions he displayed during the interaction clearly indicated—"

"Here," Silence cut him off, pointing at a door. "216."

Harvey took his card from his pocket. "You know, the historical development of hotel key systems is actually quite interesting. The transition from traditional mechanical keys to magnetic strips involved a complex evolution of security protocols that—"

"Goodnight, Harvey."

"If you consider the geometric implications of traditional lock mechanisms, there's a fascinating correlation between..."

Silence shut the door on him.

He stood in the darkness for a moment, letting the quiet wash over him.

Then, from the other side of the door connecting the adjoining rooms: "Oh! Did you know that the standard hotel room layout was established in 1957 by a committee that—"

"*Goodnight, Harvey!*"

Pain in his throat. He swallowed.

A pause.

"Right. Goodnight."

Footsteps, receding. Then, the squeak of mattress springs.

Silence sighed—"Shit..."—then shrugged off his jacket and crossed the room. Even in the dim light, he could tell the furnishings were modern, high-end, carefully selected. He stopped at the window, pulled back the blackout curtains.

It had gotten darker outside, just a bit of pinkish glow left in the sky. Streetlights and headlights aglow. From here, he could still see the pawnshop. The argument had ended, but the young man remained in the vicinity, pacing the sidewalk, running his hands through his hair in obvious distress.

Through the adjoining door, Silence heard a faint sound. His hearing was excellent. He'd been trained for it.

He approached the door.

It was a rustling sound. Paper.

More triangles, no doubt.

It struck Silence then: this was what Harvey did in his downtime. He folded more paper triangles. Silence pictured Harvey back in that criminally underutilized loft apartment in Pittsburgh, on any given day, alone with his files and his air plant, folding a day's worth of receipts.

Silence had met many strange people, but Harvey was among the strangest. It suited Harvey's job, though—logistics analyst. As Silence thought about it now, he was struck by the similarity between the Pittsburgh mission two years ago and this side mission in Wisconsin.

Like Layne Grosicki, Harvey had involved himself in trouble that wasn't his. Like Layne Grosicki, Harvey had gotten involved after finding discrepancies in official paperwork.

Had Silence not gotten there just in time—on that final day in Pittsburgh two years earlier, after Harvey's compromised boss had lured him into a cartel trap—Harvey wouldn't now be alive.

Now, history had repeated itself. If Silence hadn't arrived at Harvey's loft just in time this morning, Harvey would be dead at the hands of cartel hitmen.

Silence thought about how Harvey had almost gotten them both killed two years ago. It had been foolish. Reckless. But Harvey had had the best intentions.

And Harvey had been crestfallen when Silence derided those intentions after they both survived.

This morning, during the rescue, Silence had seen some of that hurt still there in Harvey's guileless eyes...

...two years later.

Silence dropped into the room's lone chair. Firm cushion, quality fabric. His mind went to the upcoming task, coming later that night—an invitation-only event at a rough pool hall run by the most criminally connected man in town. He would have to walk in as an out-of-towner with a face that didn't belong and a voice like a rock tumbler.

Simple.

A soft knock at the adjoining door.

"Clay?" Harvey's voice was muffled. "I'm a tad uncomfortable over here. The layout of things... leaves much to be desired. There's this organizational theory about feng shui in hotel rooms that..."

Silence closed his eyes.

He wondered if the young man from the pawnshop wanted to trade places.

CHAPTER FOURTEEN

For a few amazing moments, Silence had experienced a bit of peace.

Back at the upscale hotel, alone in his room, he'd immersed himself in the quiet, splaying out on the king-sized bed. Plush carpet, crisp sheets, the hum of climate-controlled air. No noise. No interruptions.

Because on the other side of the adjoining door, Harvey had fallen asleep.

For a brief while, Silence had been surrounded by comfort.

That was over now.

He was back into the pits of depravity, where his line of work often took him. The kind of places where the air stank of desperation, spilled liquor, and sweat.

Places like Kick Shot Pool Hall in Plymouth, Wisconsin.

It was a run-down dive tucked away on a side street. A buzzing neon sign—dull red—flickered erratically above the door. The sound of rock music and dozens of voices grew louder as he approached, as did the smell of body odor, stale beer, and several different kinds of smoke, all mixed together.

He had left Harvey back at the hotel. Asleep.

There was no way around it. When Doc Hazel had assigned him this job, Silence had argued that dragging a protectee along was a bad idea. But this was a Green Assignment, Doc Hazel had insisted. Safe. Routine.

This place was not safe.

The deeper Silence dug into the matters at Plymouth, the more he believed Doc Hazel had been wrong. This was no Green Assignment.

And he further realized that Joanne might be right—Layne Grosicki may well have been murdered.

Either way, bringing Harvey into a pool tournament hosted by a guy widely considered the town's top criminal wasn't wise.

Besides, Silence only had one invitation.

He stood in a short queue at the entrance, watching the scene inside unfold through dirt-smeared windows.

But he heard it more than he saw it.

The pool hall was alive with noise.

Clinking billiard balls. Laughter—some friendly, some not. The hum of a jukebox pushing out an old Fogerty tune. Locals crowded around rickety pool tables, drinks in hand, bets exchanged with casual confidence.

And there was Wayne Durante, moving through it all like he owned the place. Because he did.

Silence recognized him from the photos that he'd gotten back at the hotel business center via his Watchers information retrieval request. Late forties. Rugged, built like a guy who'd won more fights than he'd lost. Thick arms, rough hands. Five o'clock shadow, likely a permanent staple. A dark, lopsided grin that also looked permanent.

He collected bets, whispered side deals, exuded control. He laughed, clapped a guy on the back, then turned on his heel and scared the hell out of another man with just a look. Charm and menace, seamlessly blended.

Silence was dressed for the setting, but he'd kept it in line with his tastes—dark, simple, intentional.

A black, well-fitted bomber jacket over a charcoal button-up, sleeves casually rolled. Black jeans, not designer—Levi's—but clean, sharp. On his feet, black leather boots, scuffed just enough to blend in.

No tie. No flash. Just understated monochrome. Enough to look like he belonged.

In a place like this, he still stood out. But that was part of the play.

When it was his turn at the door, he handed over Caruso's invitation to the burly bouncer standing guard.

The man wore an ill-fitting jacket over a stained white T-shirt, a cigarette dangling from his lips as he glanced at the card.

"Wait a minute," the bouncer said, eyeing Silence, "this is Caruso's invite. That new guy in town. Food inspector or somethin'. I seen him talking to Wayne just yesterday. What the hell you trying to pull here?"

Silence nodded. "Stuart gave it..." He swallowed. "To me."

The bouncer hesitated. But was too tired or lazy to protest further. "Whatever, man. Just don't start trouble. Mr. Durante don't like troublemakers." He stepped aside.

Silence entered.

Inside, dim lighting cast shadows on copious pool tables —numbered for the tournament with handwritten paper signs—and a long bar area in the back. The air was thick with smoke, and now that he was engulfed in it, Silence detected the mixture better than he could outside; there was as much pot in here as tobacco. He'd be lucky to get out without a contact high.

He moved through the crowd, blending in, watching.

That wretched bar stretched along the far wall—dull black, sticky with spilled drinks, stools wobbling with every shift of weight. Beyond it, a back hallway led toward restrooms and a door labeled *PRIVATE*.

Durante moved from group to group, exchanging jokes, slapping shoulders, occasionally switching to low-voiced conversations that looked far more serious.

Silence took his time, letting the room's rhythm settle around him.

Then, an opportunity.

Durante's easygoing mood fractured for a moment. A heated exchange at the bar—sharp words, stiff posture. He leaned in, barked something at a man on a stool who looked exceedingly drunk, even for the environment.

Then, Durante turned and stormed off.

Straight down the hallway, toward the office.

Silence saw his chance.

He drifted away from the crowd toward the restrooms. Entered the men's room.

He'd noted from his initial sweep of the hallway that only a thin wall separated the men's room from Durante's office.

Silence stepped toward a stall and threw the door open.

Inside, a small, biker-looking guy jerked upright in surprise, hunched over the toilet paper dispenser. A thin white line of coke stretched across the metal surface. He wore an almost comically cliché black leather vest, stringy hair hanging over his face.

"What the hell, man?"

Then he registered the cold, unreadable look in Silence's eyes before his gaze traveled south, taking in the sheer size of the man invading his stall.

A long, tense beat.

Then the biker quickly swept his coke back into a plastic

baggie, shoved it into his pocket, and shuffled past Silence without another word nor another look in the eye.

Silence stepped inside, latched the door, and put his ear to the wall.

Listened.

Muffled voices.

"...which means you kick that asshole out," Durante's gravelly voice said, irritation clear, "if he pulls any more shit. There's enough to deal with here."

Another voice, deep and old, like a dying bear, said, "There's something else. Some guy's here using Caruso's invitation."

"Who?"

"Stuart Caruso," Bear Voice said. And after a long beat of no response from Durante, he continued, "He's that guy you were talking to the other day."

"Oh, shit, yeah. Why the hell would I care if someone else uses his invite? Didn't want that sissy here anyway."

"Who's Caruso?"

"Some food inspector. He's out of Milwaukee, like the guy who died. Gosetti. Gokowski. Whatever the hell his name was. The food inspector was following up on what the other guy was asking about. Something about... rotten batches of cheese or some such shit. I got no clue. Asking all sorts of questions about McCrorie. Ya know, that scarred-up piece of shit."

Silence stilled.

Durante had no idea who Layne Grosicki was.

The guy may have been some kind of low-level criminal mastermind in Plymouth.

But he wasn't Silence's guy.

Silence did, however, gather a new piece of intel. A name: McCrorie. Someone Layne had been looking into. And a description of McCrorie: "scarred-up."

Silence had heard enough. He left the bathroom.

Out of the hallway, back into the thick of the pool tournament. Clacking pool balls. Shouts. Laughter. Sloshing beer.

And there was the little cokehead he'd scared out of the bathroom stall...

...talking to two of Durante's men.

Damn snitch.

Durante's men watched Silence, eyes sharp, tracking him. They moved into the crowd, coming in his direction.

Silence stepped outside. The neon sign puttered above, casting a crimson glow over his shoulders. At the corner, a trio of women paused mid-drag, eyes flicking his way.

The parking lot was packed now. Cars crammed into every space. The party had spilled past the walls of the pool hall, bodies leaning against hoods, laughter and music rolling through the humid night air.

There was the sound of the door opening again behind him.

Then footsteps followed him into the darkness.

Silence turned the corner.

The alley beside the pool hall was narrow—brick and shadow, lit by a single sodium lamp at the far end. Vomiting trash bins lined one wall, their contents spilling onto the asphalt. Above, a rusted fire escape creaked.

Shadows appeared from behind Silence, coalescing into human forms.

"Hey, Mr. Black," one of the men said.

Silence instinctively looked down at his attire—all black.

He turned to face them.

Two men materialized from the gloom.

The first was a hulking figure in a leather jacket. Brass knuckles glinted dully in the weak light.

The second was leaner. Wiry. An unlit cigarette dangled from his lips. He pulled a switchblade from his pocket. The blade snapped open with a click that echoed off the alley walls.

"You're a real troublemaker," Switchblade sneered. "Mr. Durante don't like troublemakers."

"So I heard," Silence said.

The men froze at the sound of Silence's voice. Remained like this for a moment. Then they moved, together and fast, spreading out to flank him.

Silence moved faster.

The hulking one lunged first, brass knuckles whistling through the air—but Silence was already inside his reach, twisting. The brass knuckles flew past his face and clanked into brick. A scream.

Silence drove a sharp elbow into the man's ribs. The impact drove the air from his attacker's lungs in an explosive grunt. He stumbled backward, boots scraping.

The lean one slashed with the knife. Silence sidestepped, caught the man's wrist, and twisted hard. The sound of tendons straining preceded the clatter of the blade on asphalt.

A precise strike to the jaw dropped him.

The first attacker tried to regain his footing, fury replacing surprise on his face—but Silence's boot found his chest, launching him backward.

The man hit the pavement hard. He slid on his ass through a puddle before coming to unceremonious rest among scattered garbage.

The alley was still then. Silence's attackers groaned but made no further effort to stand.

Silence adjusted his jacket, smoothing out wrinkles that hadn't been there moments before.

He left.

CHAPTER FIFTEEN

THE PEN in Joanne's hand paused mid-sentence. Her words just weren't flowing like they had been. It was 10:30 at night. Maybe she was just too tired.

She leaned back in her chair, thoughts drifting as she stared at the last line she'd written in the journal.

The creak of the bathroom door pulled her attention. She looked up to see Clay emerging, rubbing his hands together.

Harvey, meanwhile, was at the suite's kitchenette, inspecting the complimentary coffee selection—arranged neatly around the coffee maker beside the fridge—with mild dismay.

"This is barely coffee," Harvey muttered, holding up a packet of house blend. "More like a coffee-flavored beverage. I'm disappointed in a place this nice. The standard ratio of soluble coffee solids in instant packets is—"

"Harvey," Clay cut in, his voice flat.

Harvey held up his hands. "Right, right. Not the time."

Clay walked to the suite's small dining table and took a seat across from Joanne.

They'd decided that Joanne's suite would be a suitable

meeting place, a command central of sorts. More comfortable than Clay and Harvey's adjoining rooms and more private than the lobby.

The hotel was part of a high-end national chain, and the suite smelled faintly of new carpet and fresh paint. The sleek furniture, muted colors, and modern design were pleasant and welcome surprises. Joanne rarely expected chain places to feel comfortable, let alone stylish, let alone in a tiny burgh like Plymouth.

When Clay had entered the suite with Harvey earlier—having just returned from the pool tournament and having found Harvey awake and waiting for him upon his return to the hotel—he'd given the space an approving nod, an appreciation that was subtle but noticeable. Joanne thought she might have even caught the faintest hint of a smile. From his clothing and the way he carried himself, she'd been able to tell immediately that this was a man of understated but consummate style.

As Joanne closed her leather journal, she caught Clay looking down at it, a hint of curiosity playing across his granite face. He'd surely noticed how she kept the journal close at all times. He'd surely wondered what it was about.

She saw movement in his eyes as he read the cursive font branded across the front cover:

YOUR PAST
IS NOT YOUR FUTURE

When he looked up at her and made eye contact, Joanne quickly changed the subject by gesturing to Layne's letter, which was sitting on the glass tabletop a few inches from her journal. She'd torn a few pages out of the journal for note-taking, and they sat next to the envelope—scribbled in frustration, crossed out here, circled there, analyzing every possible angle to the cryptic underlined letters: *T, R, A, R, I, N.*

She hadn't reached any conclusions.

She slid the journal aside and pointed to the notes. "Any new thoughts?"

Clay pulled the sheets of paper closer, studied them. Then he picked up Layne's letter. He didn't respond.

The room was silent for a moment, save for the occasional rustle of paper.

Harvey, uncharacteristically quiet, sat nearby, looking at his lap, his hands busy with something. It took Joanne a moment to realize what he was doing—folding a piece of paper.

Perhaps Harvey was an origami aficionado. That wouldn't have surprised Joanne. It seemed to fit him.

Then—

Clay straightened.

His demeanor shifted in an instant. Eyes sharp.

Just as quickly, his expression darkened a fraction.

"Dammit."

Joanne leaned closer. "What is it?"

"I should've seen this..." he said and swallowed. "Sooner."

"You figured it out?"

Clay nodded. "It's an ROT13 cipher."

He pointed at the list of Layne's underlined letters she'd written out at the top of one of the sheets of paper: *T, R, A, R, I, N.*

Harvey bounded over. "Oh! I love ciphers! ROT13s are one of the simplest types. It's actually a version of the Caesar cipher, which—"

"Harvey," Joanne and Clay said in unison.

Harvey mouthed a sheepish "right" and retreated a step.

Joanne turned back to Clay, tilted her head. "ROT13? What's that?"

Clay didn't answer directly. Instead, he pulled one of the loose sheets closer and wrote for a moment. When he was done, he slid the paper to her.

He'd written the alphabet in two rows, the first thirteen letters directly above the second thirteen. He'd drawn a double-headed arrow in the space between the top row's first letter and the bottom row's first letter—*A* and *N*.

Farther down, he'd written Layne's underlined letters out as a word, *TRARIN*, and beneath that, another word, *GENEVA*, vertically aligning each word's six letters and drawing double-headed arrows for each.

A B C D E F G H I J K L M
↕
N O P Q R S T U V W X Y Z

T R A R I N
↕ ↕ ↕ ↕ ↕ ↕
G E N E V A

Harvey cleared his throat, a grin tugging at the corner of his mouth. "An ROT13 cipher—basically, you take the alphabet and cut it in half. The top half of letters substitutes for the bottom half and vice versa. So A becomes N, B becomes O, and so on."

She could tell Harvey was itching bad to go into further explanation—the cipher's origins, perhaps, or its use in historical context—but he restrained himself.

Joanne stared at that word—*GENEVA*. The name sat there, staring back at her.

"Okay, so we've got a word—*Geneva*," she said, frowning. "What does that mean? Why would Layne...?"

Clay didn't respond. He was looking to the side, thinking.

Harvey tapped his chin, intrigued. "There are quite a few possibilities! Geneva, Switzerland, of course. There's a play called *Geneva* by George Bernard Shaw. Then there's a steel mill out in Utah. Geneva Steel. Founded during World War II to increase American steel production, leading to—"

"No!" Clay said, jumping to his feet, startling both Joanne and Harvey. "Lake Geneva. A city. Less than..." He swallowed. "Two hours from here."

He made for the door.

And stopped. Stared at Joanne.

A new thought had crossed Joanne's mind. It must have shown on her face. Clay had picked up on it immediately.

"What?" Clay said.

Joanne hesitated, then sighed. "It's just... I already left Tracy that message on her answering machine."

Clay blinked. "And?"

Joanne frowned, staring at the cipher Clay had written out. "And now we don't need her help."

She looked down at the paper, brow furrowed.

"I never heard back from her," Joanne continued. "I figured she wouldn't call me back. But now, I guess it doesn't matter. We figured it out without her."

The room was quiet.

Then, whispering, she added, "But... what if she does call?"

Clay didn't respond.

Harvey, though, smiled. "Then you'll get to talk to your daughter again!"

"Yeah," Joanne said with a sad scoff. "I'm sure *that* would go well."

Clay just stared at her a moment longer. Then, "I gotta go."

"To Lake Geneva?"

He nodded.

Joanne blinked. "You're... you're not going alone, are you?"

He nodded.

"Hang on, what do I do?" Harvey said.

"Stay put," Clay said, heading for the door.

Harvey huffed. "I'm always left in the hotel."

Clay didn't respond. He just rushed out the door.

CHAPTER SIXTEEN

Lake Geneva, Wisconsin

SILENCE HAD ARRIVED in Lake Geneva past midnight.

The resort town was quiet at this hour, its picturesque streets lined with darkened storefronts. The air was warm but cooling, carrying the faint scent of pine and distant charcoal embers, the remnants of barbecues long since abandoned. A light breeze stirred the trees, rustling through the stillness.

It had been a long drive.

One hour and forty-five minutes north of Plymouth. Past Milwaukee. The city lights had given way to dark, empty stretches of highway, then, eventually, to the calm, polished charm of Lake Geneva.

But Silence wasn't here for the scenery.

The last hour had been spent chasing leads in the town's underbelly. Not the tourist-friendly lakeside shops and cafes —all closed—but the bars that stayed open too late, the alleys where deals got done, the places locals didn't advertise on postcards. It had been painstaking work, but he'd pieced together some intel.

And that had led him here.

A shuttered K-Mart, sitting at the edge of a half-dead strip mall.

Silence parked the Cadillac at the edge of the lot.

The large red "K" had fallen off the sign years ago, leaving only a ghostly outline. The remaining letters hung crooked, creaking slightly in the nighttime summer breeze.

He stepped out.

No movement. No cars.

But inside, beyond a broken side door, there was noise.

Silence slipped inside, moving through the shadows.

The smell was awful—mildew, dust, the stale rot of an unloved place left to die. The cavernous space was almost empty, with stripped shelves and discarded debris littering the floor.

But in the back—near the stockroom—there were voices.

A group of rough-looking men clustered near dim, battery-powered lanterns.

They were moving crates, shifting them carefully. Too carefully. Smugglers, maybe. Or drug-runners. Something illicit.

Silence crouched behind a row of toppled shelving, watching.

A wiry guy with a crowbar peeled off from the group, moving toward the aisles.

Silence had barely shifted his weight before his boot scuffed a fallen metal shelf.

Shit.

The noise was slight.

But noticeable.

The crowbar guy froze. His head snapped toward the sound.

"Who's there?"

Silence moved first.

A quick step, a sharp pivot. The guy registered him too late.

"Hey—"

Silence slammed a forearm into his throat, grabbed the crowbar before it could be swung, and twisted it out of the man's grip. The guy gasped—half pain, half shock—before Silence's fist crushed into his temple.

He went limp instantly.

Silence caught the man before he hit the cracked linoleum. He dragged the guy into the shadows. Crouched. Listened.

The others had noticed something was off.

"Rico? You good?" one of them called.

No answer.

"Shit, go check it."

Two men grabbed makeshift weapons—a broken mop handle and a heavy wrench. They fanned out, moving cautiously.

Silence stayed low. Moved through the aisles.

The first guy passed close.

Silence stepped out, quick and clean.

One hand grabbed the guy's collar, yanked him off balance. The other drove a short, brutal punch to the ribs, knocking the wind out of him. Before the guy could recover, Silence wrapped an arm around his neck, applied pressure.

Ten seconds.

Out cold.

The last guy heard the scuffle, spun toward the noise.

"What the hell?"

Too late.

Silence closed the gap, deflected the wrench with his forearm. Stepped inside his reach. A short, sharp strike to the jaw sent the man staggering.

"It's a raid!" someone shouted from deeper in the store.

One more hit.

The man crumpled.

Silence turned toward the crates the men had been guarding. Pulled back the tarp.

Laptops. Cellular phones. Miniature televisions.

Stacks of them.

Some sort of petty theft operation.

Nothing more.

Silence exhaled. The realization hit hard.

This was small-time.

Layne's clue, *GENEVA*, had led Silence here.

But Silence had been wrong. He'd misinterpreted.

Like Harvey had said, there were many possibilities for the word *Geneva*.

This sure as hell wasn't what Layne Grosicki died for. Just stolen goods moving through the back alleys of a picture-perfect resort town.

Son of a bitch!

Silence slipped back into the shadows, moving fast, quiet. In a few moments, he'd crossed back through the macabre tangle of the abandoned chain store.

His mind churned with frustration as he stepped outside into the night air.

An hour and forty-five minutes of driving. An hour of chasing leads.

And for what?

A dead end.

He reached the Cadillac.

Behind him, voices echoed from inside the K-Mart.

"Someone's here. Rico's down!"

"Shit, grab the stuff!"

Silence didn't stick around to hear the rest.

He slipped into the driver's seat, fired up the engine, and pulled out of the lot.

He'd been wrong about *GENEVA*.

CHAPTER SEVENTEEN

Plymouth, Wisconsin

IT WAS SOMETIME in the early hours of the morning. Joanne couldn't believe she was still awake. At her age, 10 pm was a late night.

Maybe it was the intrigue keeping her awake—being part of this endeavor that had quickly morphed from a failed one-woman show into a team effort.

Or the adrenaline.

Or the twisting dread in her stomach from not knowing how her daughter had reacted to the voice message.

Really, though, she knew the answer: Harvey. He hadn't shut up since Clay left.

But now Clay was back.

Joanne studied the large man. He sat brooding on the suite's cream-colored sectional, slouched, mile-long legs splayed before him. In the dim lighting from the modern sconces, Joanne could still see the clear signs of frustration contorting the man's severe features.

Clay had just returned from following yet another dead-end lead. Lake Geneva, Wisconsin, it turned out, had no connection to the word *GENEVA* Clay had deciphered out of Layne's letter. Clay had found nothing more than a petty theft ring in the resort town, no connection to Layne or suspicious shipping manifests.

These false starts were taking a toll, wearing down even Clay's stoic persistence.

Joanne could sympathize. She had been worn thin by dead ends long before Clay and Harvey even introduced themselves.

And for the last day, they'd suffered nothing but further dead ends...

Wayne Durante, with his iron-fisted control of the town's underbelly, ruling from that dingy pool hall of his, breaking kneecaps over missed payments. But no tie to Layne.

And a wild goose chase at a city nearly two hours away.

Two strikes, and they were no closer to the shadowy forces hinted at by the *GENEVA* clue.

She was alone with Clay. Harvey had ventured to the lobby vending machine to get more Midnight Branch Licorice.

Clay pulled himself up from the sectional, moved to the glass-topped dining table, and dropped back down. He had a distant look in his eyes, as if he was staring not just at Layne's letter but through it. His fingers rhythmically tapped the glass. His typically stony facade was pulled even more taut.

Trying to switch topics out of their dismal situation, Joanne said, "It's a shame Tracy didn't call me back. Layne left the *GENEVA* clue for her, after all. But, I get it, after everything that happened between us." She paused. "I hurt her, Clay. Hurt her badly."

Well, that was stupid. Joanne had hoped to lighten the

mood by switching gears, but the first thing that came to mind was Tracy and her seeming refusal to help...

...which was itself another letdown, another failure, another dead end.

Clay looked up. Though he neither said anything nor offered any non-verbals, he maintained his attention, not turning back to the papers.

Joanne supposed that was something.

Her mind skirted around the edges of the memory, the details of what she'd done to fracture her daughter's trust—and with it, their relationship—keeping it murky, just out of sharp focus. Maybe this was deliberate, this partial amnesia, leaving her numb to the guilt with which she'd tormented herself for so long.

She sighed. "I guess I had it coming, her leaving me. Parents can be... controlling. But what I did...."

The thoughts trailed off along with her words. More partial, willful amnesia.

Besides, she couldn't live in the past...

There was a very deadly present to deal with.

"What was..." Clay said, swallowed. "The 'Speak Clearly' headband?"

Apparently, Joanne wasn't going to get to leave the past behind after all. Clay was making her dive in even deeper.

The Speak Clearly headband...

Just hearing someone else say the words aloud made her feel sick.

Sick to her stomach over the sort of human being she'd been.

"It was... something I thought was harmless at the time," she said. "Something I told myself was 'helpful.' But it wasn't. It was humiliating for Layne."

Her fingers tightened into a fist on her knee.

"Layne had a lisp as a young child. And I was impatient

with it. In class—kindergarten, mind you—I used to cut him off when he spoke, tell him to just say it right. Like he was talking like that on purpose. And then... I made it worse."

She swallowed.

"I made him wear a headband."

Clay frowned. "A headband?"

Joanne nodded. "A paper band. Right across his forehead. With 'SPEAK CLEARLY' written on it. Made him wear it every time his lisp got bad."

Clay said nothing.

Didn't need to.

She knew how despicable she'd been.

Joanne exhaled sharply. "I thought I was teaching him a lesson. Instead, I turned him into a joke. The other kids began mocking him. Mimicking the lisp. Calling him names. And now I know he wore that humiliation for years."

Clay watched her for a moment. Then he pointed to the letter. "Let's continue."

Joanne shook off the memories and leaned forward. "Without Tracy's help, that means our only option—"

Clay nodded, cutting in to finish the thought. "Is to go back..." he said and swallowed. "To Sammy Rud."

Despite being at a standstill, their minds were still in sync. That was encouraging.

But before they could strategize the next move, Clay's cellular phone rang. The sharp noise cut through the quiet that had gathered in the suite.

Clay checked the multiplex, then turned back to Joanne and said, "It's my employers."

He flipped open the phone.

"Yes. Mmm-hmm," Clay said and swallowed. "I see. Okay."

As Clay collapsed the phone and put it back in his jacket pocket, his eyes locked onto Joanne's.

"What was that about?" Joanne said.

"We can't talk..." Clay said and swallowed. "To Sammy Rud."

"What? Why not?"

"Rud's dead." Clay swallowed. "Drowned in his own cheese."

CHAPTER EIGHTEEN

The next morning

SILENCE LAY AWAKE, staring at the ceiling, his jaw clenched. A sound like a chainsaw wrestling a freight train came through the wall separating his room from Harvey's.

The snoring had started the moment they went to their respective rooms. It hadn't stopped.

He'd tried everything. Pounding on the wall. Turning up his TV. Even banging on the adjoining door. Nothing penetrated the fog of Harvey's sleep or the ungodly noise emanating from it.

Another thunderous snore rattled the lamp on Silence's bedside table.

Enough.

Silence threw off his covers, stalked to the adjoining door, and used his card key.

Inside the other room, Harvey was sprawled across the bed, one leg uncovered, one arm twisted above his head, mouth open, wild hair even wilder than usual.

"Harvey!"

The snoring continued unabated.

"*Harvey!*"

Nothing.

Silence swallowed against the pain in his throat, then grabbed a pillow and threw it at Harvey's head. The man mumbled something but didn't awaken, kept snoring.

After three more attempts to wake Harvey—including turning on all the lights and opening the curtains—Silence finally resorted to shaking the bed.

Harvey's eyes fluttered open. "Oh, hey, Clay." He yawned. "Is it breakfast time already? I'm in the mood for—"

"Shower," Silence growled.

"Just let me finish this fold," Harvey said. He grabbed a half-folded receipt from the top of a stack of triangles, which sat on the nightstand beside his wallet, keys, and Mitsy—her spiky leaves, her shiny blue porcelain dish. "The angle has to be exactly—"

"Now."

Harvey looked at him, smiled, and climbed out of bed. As he shuffled to the bathroom, still clutching his paper triangle, he continued to fold.

Silence couldn't stand the curiosity any longer.

"Why the triangles?" he found himself asking.

Harvey stopped at the bathroom door, hands paused mid-fold. A laugh. Light. Forced. "What, you've never met a man with a deep appreciation for geometric precision?"

Harvey had literally laughed off the question. But something flickered across his face. A hesitation. A shadow. Gone almost as fast as it appeared.

Silence didn't push. Just filed it away.

The bathroom door closed. A moment later, the squeak of the shower faucet.

As Silence stood there, he considered the path forward that day. Everything seemed to go through the codeword

GENEVA, but the only person who could decipher that mysterious word was in Seattle and, apparently, not going to leave.

His thoughts drifted to the relationship between Joanne and her daughter. Another broken connection. If their relationship hadn't fractured, Layne's letter would have reached its intended recipient in the first place. Tracy would be here instead of Joanne—and instead of Silence and Harvey—unraveling whatever mess the dead accountant had stumbled into.

Joanne had said she'd fractured their bond by being too controlling.

A mother's careless actions. A daughter's retreat. Years of disconnect built between them like a wall, brick by brick, until even a dead man's plea couldn't bridge the gap.

Joanne's past cruelty affecting the present.

The ripple effect. The butterfly effect.

Like ripples in a pond, spreading outward, touching distant shores we never see, Doc Hazel had said.

At the time, Silence had dismissed Doc Hazel's sentiment. Silence had assured himself that everyone was responsible for his or her choices and what they let affect them.

But now... now he wasn't so sure.

Because if Joanne's words had sent Tracy running across the country, if Layne's letter had landed in the wrong hands because of it—then maybe those ripples stretched further than he wanted to believe.

His eyes drifted toward the closed bathroom door, where steam was now escaping around the edge.

Silence had pulled Harvey out of a hellhole two years ago in Pittsburgh. Saved his life. But in the process, he'd chastised the man, a sensitive soul.

Maybe Silence's own ripples were still spreading.

From the bathroom, Harvey started singing. Something old. Really old. "Buffalo Gals."

It was going to be a long day.

The lobby was quiet save for the hum of the licorice-laden vending machine and Harvey's endless chatter about proper continental breakfast arrangement protocols.

Silence chewed a waffle greedily. He hadn't eaten enough yesterday, so now he held a pair of paper plates—doubled up as a precaution against the added weight—that had been piled high with sausage, bacon, eggs, and waffles only minutes earlier. By this point, the food was almost gone.

Upon first arrival, he'd been thrilled that this hotel offered a continental breakfast. Lots of times, nicer places like this did not.

He stood by the window, scanning the street outside while he ate. The young man from the previous evening was already back at Petes Pawn & Loan, clutching the same battered laptop.

The faded hoodie, worn-out jeans, and gaunt face—all unchanged from the night before. His sandy-blond hair stuck up at wild angles like he hadn't slept. His eyes—which, in the light of day, Silence now saw to be blue—darted nervously, scanning, searching.

He wasn't just desperate. He was drowning.

The big guy, who Silence assumed to be Pete, was back as well, blocking the doorway with his girth once more. The kid pleaded with Pete, his posture tense, shoulders hunched forward. Whatever deal he was trying to make—sell, buy, trade—meant more than just some quick cash.

"Oh no," Harvey said as he stepped up beside Silence, chewing on a bagel to which he was frowning his disapproval.

"Didn't I tell ya, Clay? Look at his micro-expressions. That's pure distress. Not anger. Something's really wrong." He stole a glance at the hotel's entrance. "Maybe we should—"

"Do *not* get involved," Silence said.

"I won't!"

Harvey pulled out his wallet, and Silence caught a glimpse inside—paper triangles were crammed in among the greenbacks. He took one triangle out, ran it along his knuckles like a poker chip.

A few minutes earlier in the hotel room, Harvey had jokingly dismissed his triangle-folding. But there was clearly more to Harvey's quasi-origami obsession than mere compulsion. Had to be. There was something in the way Harvey handled each triangle like they were anchors in a storm.

"I just think someone should help the kid. That's all," Harvey added.

Silence studied his companion's face. Harvey's attention kept straying to the window, to the scene playing out across the street.

Silence remembered Harvey asking if he'd make a good detective when they arrived in Plymouth.

The last thing he needed was Harvey playing hero.

"Don't get involved," Silence repeated. He folded the paper plates in half and shoved them into the nearby trash receptacle. "Let's go."

CHAPTER NINETEEN

Seattle, Washington

TRACY SANK into the plush armchair and wrapped her hands around a mug of chamomile tea. The warmth seeped into her fingers. She took a slow sip, hoping the ritual would calm the restless churn in her mind.

It didn't.

Mom's unexpected call the previous morning had ripped through her hard-won peace like a jagged tear in fabric. Just hearing her voice had dredged up old wounds Tracy had spent years trying to forget.

After everything she'd built, everything she'd left behind, the last thing she needed was Joanne Daley crashing back into her life. Especially with wild theories about Layne Grosicki and insinuations of murder.

Tracy knew how Mom operated—always chasing the next grand mystery, always looking outward, never inward. Never acknowledging the damage left in her wake.

Yet... there had been something different in her voice. A hesitation. A vulnerability Tracy didn't recognize.

Maybe this time, it wasn't just another obsession.

She sighed and shifted in her seat. She understood the need for closure too well. It had driven her to walk away from everything in Sacramento after the divorce with Nick. Then, later, Seattle. She had told herself distance was necessary. That space from her mother, from her past, was the only way to heal.

But despite herself, Tracy couldn't ignore the flicker of unease.

Mom was a lot of things, but she wasn't often wrong about her instincts. And the way she had said that she and her private investigator, Clay, didn't think Layne's death was an accident had struck a chord.

Tracy tried to shake it off. Couldn't.

She paced to the small window overlooking her deck and the quiet street below, wrapping her arms around herself.

She'd built a good life in Seattle. Small but solid. Photography jobs, a few steady clients, her own place. No one telling her what she could or couldn't be.

Not like before.

Not like Mom.

Tracy clenched her jaw.

For years, she had tried to forget the words Joanne used to say.

You won't make it, the bitch had said. *You'll fail, just like always.*

Tracy had tried to bury the memory of the day she found out the truth.

Her first big job. A magazine offer.

And her mother had nearly ruined it for her, nearly sabotaged Tracy's entire future.

Purposefully.

Tracy had been so stunned, so furious, she had barely spoken when she packed her bags and left. First Sacramento.

Then Seattle. Farther and farther away until even the *thought* of Morro Bay felt like a past life.

Tracy turned from the window, her throat tight.

Some wounds healed. Others sank too deep.

Yet now Mom had come back. Not with excuses or manipulation but with a request.

Not for forgiveness, but for help.

Weeks ago, Tracy would have rejected her outright. And, actually, she had. For a while.

But now, the quiet in her apartment felt different. The walls too close.

And there was Layne Grosicki... Layne had reached out to her, trusting her above anyone else after so many years.

Layne was dead now...

Tracy stared at the phone.

A breeze stirred the trees outside, breaking the stillness.

Before she could reconsider...

...Tracy grabbed the phonebook.

A few flips of the pages, and a moment later, she was on the phone.

"Yes, I'd like a seat on the next available flight to Milwaukee."

CHAPTER TWENTY

Plymouth, Wisconsin

JOANNE'S HEARTBEAT POUNDED.

Tracy's voice...

After years of silence, hearing her daughter now sent a swell of emotions crashing through her. Guilt, shame, longing—feelings as raw and real now as the day Tracy had walked away.

"Tracy, thank you," she managed, gripping the phone tightly. "I wasn't sure if you would—"

"I just landed in Milwaukee," Tracy cut in. "Where are you?"

Joanne blinked, processing. "Wait—you're here? You came?"

"I'm here for Layne," Tracy said, the sharpness in her voice unchanged. "Not for you."

Joanne swallowed past the lump in her throat. "Right. Understood."

There was a pause. Then, more measured, Tracy asked, "Where are you staying?"

"The Blackwood Grand, room 501. Top-floor suite."

From the other end of the line, Tracy scoffed. "The suite. Of course."

Joanne almost smiled. The sarcasm was a comforting familiarity, even if it was bitter.

"Tracy, listen—there's something you should know before you get here."

A beat. "What?"

"My private investigator, Clay—he was able to decipher the code in Layne's letter."

No response. A long moment stretched. Then Tracy's voice sharpened. "Then *why the hell* did I just fly all the way to Wisconsin?"

Joanne winced. "Clay deciphered the code, but that just led us to another riddle from Layne: the word *Geneva.*" She hesitated, then asked, "Do you know what it means?"

Another pause. "No."

Joanne exhaled. "Then we still need you."

Tracy didn't respond right away. Then, finally, "Fine. I'll be there soon."

Beep.

Joanne stared at the silent receiver, then set it down slowly.

The suite's living room suddenly felt too quiet.

Harvey, sitting at the kitchenette with a plate of meticulously sorted breakfast pastries, paused mid-bite. "See?" he said, chewing thoughtfully. "You got to talk to your daughter again!"

Joanne sighed. "Yeah. Sure did..."

The door opened. Clay, who had stepped into the hallway to make a call of his own to his employers, entered and immediately sensed the tension. He glanced between Joanne and Harvey, then at the phone on the table.

Without a word, he pulled out his small notebook, flipped

back the plastic cover on its spiral binding, and handed it to Joanne. There was a note scrawled in his precise handwriting.

My organization discovered a new link.

A young protégé of Layne's. Name: Arlo Ford. Worked with Layne at HarborGate Logistics in Milwaukee. Has been here at a rental home the last week trying to find out what happened to Layne. 546 Bluewater Lane.

Harvey had jogged over and read the note as well. He perked up. "Wait. So we're not the only ones chasing ghosts?"

Joanne handed the notebook back to Clay and shrugged. "Apparently not."

Harvey dusted off his hands and stood. "Well, that's exciting! Also terrifying."

Joanne exhaled. Suddenly, things felt better. Tracy would be arriving soon. And they had a new lead. Things were moving.

The dead ends, it seemed, had finally ceased.

And yet, she couldn't shake the feeling that things were about to get even more complicated.

CHAPTER TWENTY-ONE

Silence double-checked the address he'd written down as the Cadillac rolled to a stop.

546 Bluewater Lane.

The house was old but well cared for. The structure showed its age—weathered wood, a slight sag in the roofline—but everything was maintained, tended to, and kept up.

Fresh paint, clean windows. A narrow path of evenly spaced pavers led from the driveway to the door, cutting through a tidy patch of trimmed grass.

Silence climbed out of the car, quickly scanned the street, then moved up the path. He reached the door and pounded.

It swung open easily from the impact. Unlatched.

He craned his neck for a look inside.

...then his lightning-fast instincts screamed a warning.

Right in time.

A sharp shove sent him stumbling sideways, his shoulder knocking against the doorframe. He caught himself, hands bracing against the wall.

He turned just in time to see two figures explode from the shadows.

They rushed him.

A flurry of movement—quick, brutal.

The first one swung. Silence ducked. The fist sailed over his head. He came up fast, slamming an elbow into the man's gut. The guy folded with a wheeze, but Silence was already moving, twisting, catching the second attacker by the wrist.

A yank, a pivot—the second man's momentum sent him crashing into the first.

Both stumbled.

Silence didn't let them recover.

He drove a knee into one's ribs—a sharp, efficient strike that sent the guy sprawling. The other tried to lunge, but Silence sidestepped smoothly, caught the back of his shirt, and yanked him off balance.

A final strike to the jaw, and the second attacker crumpled.

Then quiet.

Silence flipped on the lights.

Two men lay crumpled on the floor.

One was young, slim, sharply dressed— pressed business attire, neatly styled black hair. Asian American, early twenties. Silence recognized him from the Specialist's description on the phone. Arlo Ford. The kid's face was twisted in pain, his brown eyes wide with confusion.

The other was shorter but powerfully built. Older, graying stubble. Hispanic. Olive complexion. He was already getting back to his feet, grumbling under his breath. A tool belt clung to his waist.

Silence stood over them and looked at the younger one. "Arlo Ford?"

The young man nodded shakily. He rubbed his jaw. "Who the hell are you?"

"Clay," Silence said.

He allowed Arlo and the older man the customary moment of stunned confusion over Silence's awful voice.

Then he added, "Private detective."

Arlo's expression shifted. "You're... here about Layne too, then?"

Silence nodded.

"How'd you find me?"

Silence didn't respond.

"So... you know I came here to find my friend."

Silence didn't respond.

Years in the field had taught him that if you stay quiet, people will fill in the blanks for you. Human nature. Predictable. And with his throat condition, it was a tendency that worked in his favor.

Arlo exhaled, rubbing the back of his neck. "Yeah. I'm in Plymouth to figure out what really happened to Layne." His voice was steady, but there was something raw underneath. "I had two weeks of vacation saved up at HarborGate, and I've almost burned through them. I need answers soon. Layne told me he found something. Something off. And that he might have gotten himself into trouble. But he still came here to Plymouth to check it out." A pause. Then, quieter, "And now he's dead. And I don't buy for a second that it was an accident."

He looked to the side for a moment.

"Layne was more than a friend. He was my mentor. Damn good dude."

A mentor. A damn good dude. The kind of man who left an impression. Enough that a young guy would burn his own time chasing the truth about his death.

Silence thought again about the ripple effect.

Then he nodded toward the older man, who was still making his way to his feet. "Who's this?"

"That's Marcos Rentería."

"Big Mark," the man added in a deep and accented voice.

"He's my temporary landlord," Arlo said. "This place is a rental. When he found out why I was in town, he insisted I stay here instead of some motel. Said I shouldn't be sleeping in a place like that." He hesitated. "He's, um... a little protective."

Big Mark snorted, adjusting his stance and his tool belt. "Damn right I am."

"Why did you..." Silence said, swallowed. "Attack?"

Earlier, during the flurry of activity after Silence pounded on the door, there had been just a fraction of a moment to put the pieces together—that it had been the older man who lunged first, followed by the younger one, who had seemed hesitant.

"Because there were men here last night," Big Mark said. "Creeping around *esta casa*. My property! Three of them. Dressed like... soldiers."

Silence turned back to Arlo. "And Layne thought..." Swallow. "He was in danger?"

Arlo shrugged. "Yeah. But he wouldn't give me specifics. Said doing so would put me in danger too, and he didn't want that."

Silence studied him. "Layne was right."

Arlo frowned. "What?"

"You could be..." Silence said, swallowed. "In danger too. Already had visitors."

Arlo exchanged a look with Big Mark.

Silence continued, "Go back to Milwaukee. My team..." Another swallow. "And I will figure this out."

Arlo's expression darkened. "No way, man. I'm staying."

Silence held Arlo's gaze for a beat, then gave a slight nod —acknowledgment, nothing more. Without another word, he turned and walked out.

CHAPTER TWENTY-TWO

Silence approached Rud's Artisanal Cheese Shop from across the street, his gaze sweeping over the darkened storefront.

It was Saturday. The place should have been open.

But it wasn't.

Two laminated signs were taped to the glass door. One was a typed message printed in bold block letters:

CLOSED UNTIL FURTHER NOTICE. THANK YOU FOR YOUR UNDERSTANDING.

Below it, a second sign, slanted and uneven, handwritten in blue Sharpie:

We miss you already, Sammy. Rest easy, friend.

Silence regarded the signs for a moment.

Then, he moved.

The alley behind the shop was quiet and empty.

Silence crouched near the back door, testing the handle. Locked. No surprise.

He pulled a rake pick from his pocket, inserted it into the cheap cylinder lock, and worked quickly.

A few flicks of his wrist, a distinct scrape.

Click.

Unlocked.

Before entering, Silence slid a powerful magnet along the door's edge, disabling the entry sensor. These consumer-level alarm systems were adequate, but for someone with the skill level of a Watchers Asset, they were simple enough to bypass if you knew where they were located—Silence had located all the sensors the previous day when he and Joanne were there. Act of habit.

Silence slipped inside, shutting the door quietly behind him.

Rud's Artisanal Cheese Shop was silent and still and surprisingly cheerful looking in the afternoon light, especially in light of the circumstances.

As he moved through the dormant equipment, Silence noticed something odd—a tarp-covered form near the front counter that seemed out of place in a cheese shop.

In the police report, Rud's death had been ruled an accident—falling into a vat while working alone after hours. But there was no way in hell that was true. Not for an experienced cheese man like Rud.

Layne Grosicki had also died in Plymouth in a supposed accident a few days earlier. Quite a coincidence for such a small town.

Silence didn't believe in coincidences.

He came to the elevated walkway where Rud had supposedly fallen. The section of railing identified as the failure point was circled by plastic police tape, which Silence lifted and ducked under. Squatting down, he inspected the metal bars, running a hand along the worn steel. A faint smear of oil. Scratches near the joints.

He leaned closer, examining the brackets and bolts. All appeared to be in order.

But he kept looking. Rising, he circled the platform, searching for anything amiss. As he reached the broken section, he spotted it—a set of bolt heads with fresh tool marks, edges stripped just enough to stand out.

Stooping to examine, Silence saw that none of the other bolt heads were marred in such a way.

He felt a tingle at the base of his neck, signaling that intuition of his that C.C. had been so proud of.

Someone had worked these bolts free.

Accident, indeed.

Whoever loosened these bolts wanted it to look like Rud had leaned too far over the railing—maybe checking a batch, maybe just careless—and lost his balance. A tragic slip, a fall into the churning cheese vat below.

But this railing hadn't failed on its own.

Which meant Rud's death was likely premeditated murder.

Silence was straightening when he caught a faint scuff behind him. He spun just as a machete sliced through the air where his head had been. Ducking reflexively, he drove forward and slammed into his attacker's midsection. They crashed to the floor in a tangle of limbs.

The man was powerfully built, with prison tattoos tracing down his thick arms. But his size made him slow.

Silence delivered a precise elbow strike to the man's temple as they grappled. The man's grip loosened enough for Silence to wrench away the machete. It fell from the walkway and clattered onto the floor below.

Both Silence and the other man scrambled to their feet.

The man lurched forward, shoulder first. But Silence was

ready. He slipped the attack, pivoting the other man face-first into the railing.

Before the thug could react, Silence had his arm torqued behind his back, inches from dislocating it. As Silence reached for the man's back pocket, the fabric tore, spilling a wallet onto the walkway.

Taking advantage of Silence's momentary loss of balance, the man pulled free and bolted down the steps and back into the shop. He ripped the tarp away, revealing a dirt bike.

Before Silence could reach him, the guy kicked the bike to life and gunned it straight through the plate glass storefront.

The crash of shattering glass was immediately followed by the piercing wail of the security alarm.

Silence's time was now severely limited.

First, he picked up the wallet. The Michigan driver's license inside belonged to one Lawrence Festin.

Hired out-of-state muscle, no doubt.

Silence sprinted to the secluded office in the back, the alarm screaming through the building.

The office was immaculate. Rud had been organized. Precise. A man who ran his business cleanly, efficiently. Not a scrap of paper out of place.

With the alarm blaring in his ears, Silence's hands moved methodically yet urgently, flipping through files and skimming over pages. He was looking for something specific—the word *GENEVA*, something that would unlock the secrets.

And he found it.

Side by side with another word.

GENEVA and *CASHMAN*.

They were together at the top of the paper, each heading a column of numbers, indecipherable to Silence. They appeared to be serial numbers of some sort.

Both words, he noted, had a clear connection to money. *Cashman* was obvious, practically spelling it out. But *Geneva* was more subtle. Geneva, the capital of Switzerland, a country synonymous with banking, wealth, and the famous—sometimes infamous—numbered accounts.

It could be about money...

It was always about money.

He had been looking at this all wrong. His previous attempt to decipher the meaning of *Geneva* had been too literal, leading him to the resort town Lake Geneva.

Maybe the key wasn't in what *GENEVA* and *CASHMAN* meant individually but in their shared structure.

With sirens wailing in the distance, he stuffed several sheets of paper in his pockets and left.

CHAPTER TWENTY-THREE

An hour later

McCrorie pulled his Dodge Ram to a stop in the alley behind Maple Street, a block from Rud's Artisanal Cheese Shop. Through the gap between buildings, he saw police cars, their lights flashing silently as officers milled around the shattered storefront. Glass glittered across the sidewalk in the late afternoon sun.

A dirt bike was propped against the alley wall beside a dumpster, its front wheel bent, fender mangled.

Killing the engine, McCrorie stepped out of the truck and surveyed the scene. The situation was worse than he'd expected.

Especially with an elite operator moving through town.

A faint groan caught his attention. In the shadow beside the dumpster, he found one of the out-of-state contractors—Festin, he believed this one's name was—hauling himself unsteadily to his feet beside the damaged bike.

Unbelievable.

These guys hadn't cost much, but their reputation had been strong.

McCrorie grabbed a fistful of Festin's shirt and slammed him back against the brick wall. "What the hell happened here?"

Festin's eyes rolled drunkenly. "Some... guy was nosing around. Tall dude, military-looking. Didn't get a name."

Shit.

It was the "private eye." Clay.

McCrorie tightened his grip, fingers twisting in the greasy fabric. "And you didn't stop him?"

"Hey, I tried, dude," Festin said. "Came at him with a machete. He was slippery though. Had to crash through the front window to get away."

With a disgusted snort, McCrorie released Festin. Sloppy idiots like this one from Michigan were what happened when you hired cheap street muscle.

But the elite cost real money, and this was supposed to be a quick, quiet cleanup job at the cheese shop with a negligible money trail and equally negligible paper trail.

"Where was he nosing around?" McCrorie said.

"He was heading for the office in the back when I jumped out at him."

Shit!

McCrorie paced the alley, mind racing over implications. Undoubtedly, the operator had sniffed out that Rud's death was no accident. That meant scrutiny, deeper digging, going through Rud's paperwork, looking for clues.

As McCrorie stomped away from the idiot Festin, leaving him swaying beside his wrecked bike, he pulled out his cellular phone and jabbed at the buttons. The line rang twice.

"Yes?" a man answered. "What goddamn catastrophe do you have to report this time?"

McCrorie kept his tone low. "We've got a problem. The supposed private eye is starting to connect the dots."

CHAPTER TWENTY-FOUR

SILENCE HAD to work up the strength to flip open his cellular phone.

The incoming call was from Doc Hazel.

"Ma'am?"

"How many of the letters have you completed?" Doc Hazel's immediate question was as clinical and probing as her voice.

Silence clenched a fist.

The letter-writing exercise—Doc Hazel's latest attempt at forcing him to process his emotions. He was meant to write three letters but never send: one to someone who wronged him, one to someone he wronged, and one to someone whose life he impacted unexpectedly.

"Two," he said and swallowed.

"Tell me about them."

"Rather not."

"This isn't optional, Suppressor! The first letter?"

Silence exhaled. "To Asset 21." He swallowed. "From the Boston mission."

"The second letter?"

"To a civilian."

"Let me guess—Missouri?"

"Yes."

"Good. That's a good one for you to process, Suppressor. And you're avoiding the third letter because...?"

"Not avoiding." Silence said, swallowed. "Mission takes priority." Another swallow. "No time."

"The third letter is crucial. Someone whose life you impacted unexpectedly. It's time you recognized the ripple effects of your actions."

Silence grunted.

"Excuse me?" Doc Hazel snapped.

Silence hadn't said a word, only grunted. But that grunt had sounded an awful lot like *Whatever*.

"Nothing, ma'am."

"Yeah. Sure. I'll be checking again, Suppressor."

Beep.

Silence set the phone down on the table in front of him.

Shuddered.

And refocused.

He was in Joanne's hotel suite where, before the phone call, he had been scrutinizing the documents he'd nabbed from Sammy Rud's Artisanal Cheese Shop. He went back to work.

Most items were invoices for cheese equipment and custom fabrication services, opaque in their engineering terminology and legalese but hinting at unusual modifications.

One scrap of paper caught his attention—another document bearing the word *CASHMAN*, this time scrawled in Rud's clumsy hand. Beneath that, Rud had written *OBSIDIAN*.

This was a name Silence knew well—Obsidian. And seeing it in the handwriting of a humble cheese shop owner from Plymouth, Wisconsin, was enough to make Silence's pulse jump.

But for now, he put aside the notion, focusing on the first puzzle piece: *GENEVA* and *CASHMAN*.

One thing at a time.

Harvey was on the sofa behind him. Napping. Snoring.

Joanne stood in the doorway with her arms crossed, observing Silence's work. The quiet between them was heavy, broken by the faint sound of paper shuffling as Silence sifted through the materials.

Joanne's anxiety radiated from her, which only added to the tension in the room. The woman's estranged daughter was in town but had not arrived at the hotel. Of course she was anxious.

Her hands fidgeted with her journal. Nervous movements. Unconscious.

Silence pointed at the journal.

He didn't need to say anything because Joanne understood his meaning. She looked down. Smiled. Not a happy smile. Something else.

She turned the journal toward him, displaying the words burned into the leather cover:

YOUR PAST
IS NOT YOUR FUTURE.

"Probably seems to you like I've had it forever," she said, "given how much I carry it around. But no. Found it a few days ago at a bookstore here in Plymouth." She ran her fingers over the branded letters. "I was getting coffee and saw it on a display by the register. The words on the cover just... spoke to me." A pause. "I haven't been a good person most of my life. I'm not young anymore, but I'm trying to make up for lost time as best I can."

Silence considered this. Nodded. And went back to work.

At the shop, Silence had realized there must be a tie between *GENEVA* and *CASHMAN*. Now, his instincts told him these weren't names of concepts but of people. The clues pointed to something larger at play in Plymouth—something that tied together Layne's murder, Rud's murder, and the investigation Layne had been conducting before his death.

Work like that took a team.

And a team needs a leader.

Silence looked up from the papers and waved Joanne over. She obliged, joining him at the table.

He pointed to Rud's note.

"If I had to bet..." Silence said and swallowed. "Geneva is a message." Another swallow. "And Cashman is a person."

"A person? Like, the leader?"

Silence nodded. He lowered his face, locking eyes with Joanne to prompt her toward the conclusion he had already reached.

"A leader..." Joanne said. "As in, the person Layne was investigating?"

Silence nodded.

"McCrorie," Joanne said.

"Right."

McCrorie had been a person of interest from the beginning before Silence arrived in Plymouth, a name Layne had been looking into, someone who Silence had confirmed to be a local via the conversation he overheard at Kick Shot Pool Hall. Silence considered the implications—McCrorie as an enforcer for powerful elements, using his local connections to enable Obsidian's enterprise.

Joanne frowned at the note on the table. "But what's Obsidian?"

Silence's voice was gruff. "Terrorist network.

International. No home base." He swallowed. "Known for random attacks." Another swallow. "With no clear patterns."

But that wasn't the half of it.

Unlike the showboating extremist groups that plastered their logos across the news, Obsidian worked in shadows so deep most intelligence agencies doubted they existed. They didn't plant bombs or hijack planes—they turned everyday systems against themselves. Water supplies. Power grids. Shipping routes. Their attacks looked like accidents, equipment failures, or natural disasters. By the time anyone realized they were under attack, Obsidian's operatives had already vanished, leaving false trails and carefully crafted dead ends.

What made them truly dangerous wasn't their capacity for violence—it was their patience. They could embed operatives for years, waiting for the perfect moment to strike. When they did, they didn't just destroy targets—they eroded faith in the institutions meant to protect them. They weaponized bureaucracy itself, turning routine inspections and safety protocols into tools of devastation.

And they never claimed credit for their work. They didn't need to. The chaos they created was reward enough.

Joanne looked up sharply. "And they're *here*?"

Silence nodded. "Looks like it."

"That's not possible," she said, shaking her head. "This is... a small city, a dairy town!"

Silence didn't argue. He let her sit with the impossibility of it for a moment.

Then, a knock at the door.

Joanne jolted.

They both looked.

Somehow, Silence knew who it must be. More of that intuition of his.

From Joanne's reaction—shaking—he knew she must have also understood who was on the other side of the door.

Silence moved to the door and opened it.

Tracy Simmons stood there, stiff as a board. Silence recognized her from the photo Joanne had shown him, but in person, she carried an edge—quiet, confident, assessing. Dark blue eyes. Chestnut hair, tied back. Fair skin, a little lined. Practical clothes.

She didn't even glance at Joanne.

Her eyes locked onto Silence instead. "You must be Clay?"

Silence nodded.

Tracy hesitated. Her breath caught for half a second as she absorbed the sound of his voice. Then, she shook it off, extending a hand. "I'm Tracy."

Silence shook her hand, then stepped aside to let her in.

Tracy entered stiffly. Still didn't look at Joanne.

Harvey, who had apparently woken from his nap, suddenly sprang up. "And I'm Harvey King!"

Tracy blinked at him.

Then, something happened that Silence wasn't expecting.

She smiled. A small thing. Almost reluctant. Like her face hadn't made the expression in a long time.

Harvey grinned at the response, bouncing slightly on his feet. "You like cheese? You're in the cheese capital of the world, ya know. I can give you some recs. A good cheddar can solve a lot of problems, I always say."

Tracy gave a slight shake of her head, the smile already fading, as she turned back to Silence. "I heard you already solved the code, Clay."

Silence retrieved Layne's letter and the PenPal notebook—flipping to the page where he had written the word *GENEVA*—and handed them both to her.

Tracy took the letter, her fingers pressing over the words as she read. A bittersweet smile ghosted across her lips.

"A ROT13 cipher led to this word," Silence said, tapping the notebook.

Tracy lingered on Layne's letter a moment longer, then looked away. Stunned. Her fingers tightened slightly around the envelope.

Silence considered the fact that she and Layne had been childhood friends.

Joanne inhaled sharply as if about to say something.

Tracy didn't acknowledge her.

Instead, she shook her head, pulling herself back into the moment. "I can't think of what Geneva might mean."

Silence said nothing.

Tracy exhaled, gaze unfocused. For a moment, she just stared at the far wall, lost in thought.

Then—her eyes lit up.

She turned sharply to Silence.

"Wait! When we were kids, Layne and I used to play this game. We'd pretend to be spies, Cold War sort of stuff, making up codes and passwords. One of them was *Geneva*."

Silence raised a brow. "Why Geneva?"

"It started with this history phase we went through," Tracy said, nostalgia flavoring her voice. A smile. "We'd read about the Geneva Convention and the Geneva Protocol, and Layne loved pointing out how people always confused the distinction between the two. It was an inside joke between us. I know, I know. We were nerds."

"The Geneva Protocol," Silence said, swallowed. "Banned chemical and biological weapons."

Tracy nodded. "Yeah. A lot of times people think they're banned in the Geneva *Conventions*, but there's a distinction between the Conventions and the Protocol." She paused. "Anyway, yeah, I remember specifically talking about this as a kid with Layne. He must have been trying to tell us something about biological weapons."

Silence straightened. His mind spun, fitting the pieces into place.

Biological weapons...

Tainted cheese shipments.

Silence's mind raced.

"That's what..." he said, swallowed. "Layne was trying to tell you!"

Tracy cocked her head. "Huh?"

"Biological weapons," Silence said and swallowed, his gaze shifting over the other three in turn. "Embedded in cheese." Another swallow. "Shipped out of Plymouth... to anywhere. *Obsidian*."

They finally had a real lead.

CHAPTER TWENTY-FIVE

THROUGH THE HOTEL lobby's picture windows, Silence watched the young man at the pawnshop across the street trying unsuccessfully to sell the laptop to Pete. This was the third time he'd seen the young man. Same desperate gestures, same pleading posture.

He turned away, settling into one of the vinyl chairs in the breakfast area. A few moments ago, he and Harvey had left the suite upstairs, giving Joanne her moment alone with Tracy after years of estrangement.

Silence doubted it was going well.

Tracy had barely looked at her mother when she arrived. Hadn't said a word to her. It didn't seem like the kind of reunion that led to tearful embraces.

He let the thought go. There were more important matters with which to occupy his brain space. He glanced down at his PenPal on the table. Three sets of words he'd written in all caps:

OBSIDIAN

BIOLOGICAL WEAPONS

MCCRORIE IS THE KEY

A few moments earlier, he'd speed-dialed Watchers Specialists with another information retrieval request looking for any known haunts of someone named McCrorie in Plymouth, Wisconsin. Wherever the man operated, Silence needed to know.

Across from him, Harvey sat hunched over a Wisconsin Dairy Producers Monthly, flipping through the pages with exaggerated focus. He muttered to himself, voice low, rhythm steady.

"You ever read one of these? Some guy in here's arguing about the moisture content of an Alpine-style Gruyère. Like, fighting mad about it. Pages of angry letters."

Silence barely registered it. His mind was elsewhere.

Obsidian.

Not a typical terrorist outfit. No bombings. No demands. No glory-seeking. They operated in the shadows, embedding operatives deep within systems, taking years to execute attacks. When they did strike, it looked like something else—a corporate failure, a public health crisis, a bureaucratic meltdown. Untraceable. Impossible to pin down. Psychological and economic warfare at its finest. They didn't just hit institutions. They rotted them from the inside.

And now, they were here.

Silence had reached a conclusion that had settled into his gut with the weight of certainty. Obsidian was using the city of Plymouth like a massive tool. Transporting biological weaponry via the town's cheese shipments. It made too much sense.

This was what Layne had uncovered.

Of course, among the first people Layne had contacted was Sammy Rud. But Rud was dead. Murdered.

Obsidian, of course.

Cleaning up their mess.

Harvey flipped a page, shaking his head. "Some guy won Best Artisan Brie three years in a row, and now people are writing in, claiming the judges are biased. Cheese corruption. Who knew?"

Silence kept his eyes on the notebook.

McCrorie.

The local muscle. If Silence found him, he found his way to the next link in the chain.

Which made him think of another word that had come up during the investigation...

CASHMAN.

That would be the *true* leader, not McCrorie.

Silence finally looked up, found Harvey flipping through the magazine with one hand, folding a gas station receipt in his other.

Silence gestured at the receipt. "The triangles."

Harvey's fingers froze mid-fold. "Oh, you know me. I just like things orderly." He glanced at the neat stacks of magazines, then added, "Did you know the ancient Egyptians actually used triangular—"

"Harvey."

Harvey had tried to deflect with a joke again. Silence wasn't going to allow it. Not this time.

"Tell me about..." Silence continued, swallowed. "Triangles."

"It's..." Harvey's voice came out softer than usual. "It's my mom."

He reached for his wallet, carefully handling it as if it held something more than IDs and credit cards.

"She used to write me little messages. *I love you.* Or, *You're doing great.* Or, *Have a good day*. Things like that. She folded them up. Always triangles." His fingers traced the edge of one. "She died when I was fifteen."

Silence didn't respond.

"She used to say..." Harvey swallowed. "She said if she gave me one triangle, I could make another. Together, the two would form a heart." He pulled out two folded scraps of paper and placed them on the table, overlapping them to form a roughly heart-like shape. "See? One's hers, one's mine. Together, we're whole."

Silence studied him. All the triangles over the past few days. Dozens, probably, folded absentmindedly in cars, in hotel rooms, on diner counters. Not just a habit. A coping mechanism. A comfort.

They were halves of hearts.

Harvey cleared his throat, voice suddenly lighter. "Anyway. Just a thing I do."

Silence didn't respond. Just nodded.

Harvey shifted in his seat, then glanced at the window. Pete was gone, but the young man was still there, slumped against the pawnshop's brick wall, looking defeated, laptop hanging low at his side.

"I, uh..." Harvey stood. "I need some air."

Silence glanced out the window at the pawnshop, then back to Harvey. "Don't get involved."

"I won't." Harvey wouldn't meet his eyes. "Just need to stretch my legs."

He left.

Silence watched him go—out the automatic doors and into the sunlight. Despite the moment they'd just shared, despite understanding Harvey's fragility more now than he had before, he still felt relief.

The void Harvey left in his absence was always relieving.

Silence observed Harvey's performance through the window. The man made a show of walking in the opposite direction of the pawnshop, even checking his watch like he had somewhere to be. Then, when he thought he was out of sight, he looped around.

Silence shook his head, sighed.

On the table, the two triangles still lay where Harvey had placed them, overlapped into a harsh-edged heart. Silence pocketed them. He would return them to Harvey later.

He turned back to the window. Harvey was closing in on the kid with the laptop, hunching his shoulders as though this would somehow keep him out of Silence's line of sight.

Silence sighed again.

Harvey could very well get himself into some trouble over there. But probably not much. At worst, the laptop guy would sob story him into forking over some cash.

And either way, it got Harvey out of Silence's hair for a while.

Sure, Harvey was his protectee. But despite Harvey's childlike tendencies, he wasn't a child. He was a grown man. He could take care of himself—for a little while, at least.

Things were ramping up in Plymouth. Getting more dangerous by the hour. A Harvey reprieve was a good thing.

Silence's cellular phone buzzed.

He glanced at the LCD multiplex display. The Watchers.

Silence grinned.

He was about to get some damn answers.

Finally.

CHAPTER TWENTY-SIX

THE CLOCK in the kitchenette ticked.

Joanne sat motionless on the hotel suite's armchair, staring at nothing. The thick drapes smothered the daylight, leaving the room in a dim, muted haze.

For the last several minutes, she had simply existed—not moving, barely breathing, just listening to the ticking.

After Clay and Harvey had left, she had tried. Really tried.

She had faced Tracy, reached out—not physically, but with words, an attempt to bridge the years that had stretched too far, made them strangers. But Tracy had refused to respond, had barely acknowledged Joanne was even in the room.

Several minutes passed in quiet before Tracy finally spoke.

Still without looking at Joanne.

"Now that Clay has deciphered the letter and figured out what Geneva really meant, there's no reason for me to be here," Tracy had said. "But if I am, I might as well explore the 'Cheese Capital of the World' before I fly back to Washington."

She had walked to the door.

Joanne had called after her.

"Tracy..."

But Tracy hadn't stopped. Hadn't turned. The door thudded shut behind her.

Now, Joanne sat alone in the quiet, her mind looping through old memories.

Tracy as a child. Bright-eyed. Always moving, always asking questions. Always with a camera slung around her neck by the time she was ten, snapping pictures of things no one else noticed—clouds curling in the afternoon sky, the cracked pavement outside the grocery store, a lost mitten on a park bench.

She had loved that girl so much. Still loved her. Of course.

But the girl she loved wasn't there anymore. In her place was a hardened woman with sharp eyes and clipped words and a posture that bristled if Joanne so much as stepped too close. The woman who had been the girl who had been Joanne's daughter had a few wrinkles now. Even a couple of grays. Time had changed her.

Time had changed Joanne, too.

She had done a lot in the last few years to be better. To not be the person she once was—the controlling, cruel mother. The terrible kindergarten teacher who had no business shaping young minds.

How had she ever thought she belonged in a classroom?

She felt the weight of it all now. The guilt.

She had spent decades being awful. The kind of person who shouldn't be forgiven, who shouldn't expect to make amends. How could you undo something like that? How could you fix a past that had been broken for so long?

A tap at the door.

Her heart surged. Hope—stupid, desperate hope—rushed into her chest.

"Yes?"

The door swung open.

Not Tracy.

It was Clay.

Joanne exhaled. The hope in her chest collapsed back into its usual emptiness.

Clay scanned the suite, his eyes flicking toward the closed bedroom door, taking in the dark emptiness save for Joanne. He said nothing.

Joanne answered his unasked question. "She went out to explore Plymouth."

Clay turned his gaze to her. He didn't respond. Didn't need to. She saw it in his eyes—pained pity.

Joanne squared her shoulders and changed the subject. "Where's Harvey?"

Clay blinked. "Also exploring..." he said and swallowed. "Plymouth."

He pulled his small notebook from his pocket and gave it a shake.

"I have..." He swallowed again. "A new lead."

CHAPTER TWENTY-SEVEN

JOANNE SAT in the passenger seat of Clay's silver Cadillac STS as he drove them down a narrow, winding road through the dense Wisconsin forest. They were somewhere between the motel and Plymouth, heading toward an address Clay had unearthed. The road was tight, with towering trees creating a natural tunnel that blocked most of the sunlight.

On Joanne's lap was the stack of papers Clay had taken from the cheese shop, and on top was the page he'd told her to examine. He had circled an address—a remote spot in the trees. That's where they were going.

"What is this place?"

"Address was written in the papers..." Clay swallowed. "From Rud's office." Swallowed. "My people cross-referenced it." Another swallow. "It has ties to McCrorie."

Joanne shrugged. "Fair enough."

Clearly, this address was a slender thread in Clay's investigation, a thread that now tied back to this McCrorie individual he'd heard about. Everything pointed to McCrorie as a key figure... but not the elusive Cashman, the shadowy puppet master pulling strings for Obsidian's operations in Wisconsin.

That person was yet to be found.

A wave of surrealism came crashing in.

Joanne's partnership with Clay had happened on a whim, a decision made in the fleeting moment in the hotel lobby. The pairing had been jarring—especially with Clay's unorthodox methods and mechanical demeanor.

But as the investigation unfolded, a sense of comfort had crept in. Because something about Clay reminded Joanne of Tracy.

It wasn't a physical resemblance—tall, imposing Clay was laughably disparate from her daughter—but something more profound, a shared precision, a careful way of observing the world. In a way, it gave Joanne hope.

The dusty road abruptly stopped at a sagging chain-link gate, its edges laced with razor wire. Beyond the gate stood a desolate metal structure, possibly an abandoned warehouse or workshop. Time had worn down the corrugated metal siding to a dull, ashen color. Graffiti on the walls, the roof. The sound of chains rattling was carried by the wind as it gusted through the surrounding trees.

Clay parked.

"Stay here," Clay said.

Joanne shook her head. "I want to see this through with you, Clay. All of it."

Clay stared back at her.

Sure, Joanne was making changes rapidly, working her ass off at being a better human being. But she could still dip into the stubborn old bitch persona when it suited her, couldn't she?

Finally, Clay shrugged and stepped out of the car.

Joanne followed.

They made their way toward the building. The main door

was slightly ajar, scraping against dirt as they pushed it open farther. Inside, the space was dark and vast, with a floor made of raw earth and steel pillars supporting the roof. Spiderwebs hung from the ceiling. Shadows devoured corners atop piles of wooden crates. The air smelled musty, damp.

No sign of recent human habitation. But the thread had led here for a reason.

Joanne's palms were slick with sweat. Her stomach churned. She had to remind herself that she'd *insisted* on coming in here.

But as Clay stood beside her, radiating calm and assurance, she felt a confidence grow within herself. She followed Clay's lead. He moved quietly, senses alert.

Ten yards in, a flurry of motion exploded out of the murk.

Figures lunged at them, men wielding knives and lengths of pipe, their eyes wild. Four of them.

Not a situation to walk into unprepared.

But Clay was prepared.

Of course.

As the first attacker lunged, Clay's reaction was a fluid surge of motion. He pivoted on the balls of his feet, arm shooting out, fingers stiff, striking a throat. The man stumbled back, clawing at his neck, wheezing.

Strong hands gripped Joanne's arms—firmly but not roughly, some sort of distorted chivalry offered to an older woman. A calloused palm pressed over her mouth, stifling her cry.

Meanwhile, Clay shot through the swarm of attackers. A powerful elbow collided with a nose, producing a loud crunch. A palm struck a chest with a whooshing impact. His leg moved in a blur as it connected with a man's knee, cracking it. The man bellowed.

Finally, he reached Joanne's captor. A fist came in her direction. She screamed, closed her eyes...

...and somehow it was over.

The man's hand flew from her face. She could no longer feel him pressed up behind her.

She opened her eyes.

The man was on the dirt floor. They were all on the floor.

Clay stood tall, his chest rising and falling, winded but not breathless. The other men whimpered in the dirt.

The biggest of the men—the one in a light blue denim shirt, the one who'd tried to restrain Joanne—blinked up at Clay and managed to grind out, "You with that other guy? The one who was here before?"

"You mean Layne Grosicki?" Joanne said.

The guy blinked for a moment, then, "Yeah. Yeah, that sounds right.

"Layne was..." Clay said, swallowed. "Here?"

The man's face shifted. A flicker of realization—he'd said too much. His gaze dropped, turning away from Clay's stare.

Clay grabbed a handful of the man's denim shirt and yanked him off the floor.

He slammed the man into the wall.

"*Talk!*" Clay growled in his face.

"Okay, okay!" the man cried. "Take it easy!" He gulped, then words came out in a tumbling rush. "Julian McCrorie has been using this place to store specialty cheese shipments. That's it, man! Just storage. He's working for this... group. Obsidian. And some guy called the Cashman. All we do is hide the stuff in those boxes for McCrorie!" He pointed with his chin toward the crates.

While Clay kept the squirming man pinned against the wall, Joanne stepped over to the crates and pulled back one of the tops. The lid fell off and clattered in the dirt, throwing up a dust cloud.

Empty.

"We ain't got anything now!" the man said. "McCrorie and

his guys came and took the stuff last week. They're ramping things up. Got eyes everywhere in town. Getting ready for... whatever it is they're doing tonight."

With that last word, *tonight*, Joanne and Clay exchanged a glance.

Another phrase the man said stuck out in her mind. *Got eyes everywhere in town.*

Joanne wondered if she'd been followed the entire time she'd been in Plymouth. She and Clay both. Which made her also think of...

...Tracy.

"So if you're here because of Arlo, I'm sure the kid's safe now," the man continued. "I mean, now that the Grosicki guy is dead, they're not gonna need Arlo."

"What are you..." Clay said and swallowed, stepping right into the man. "Talking about?"

The man cowered. "They were going to use the kid... as bait. To draw out that Layne guy tonight. But now with that guy dead, the kid's gotta be safe."

Joanne touched Clay's arm. "Or he's in more danger than ever! And Tracy, too!"

Clay must have agreed because, because without a word, he turned and strode toward the exit. Joanne chased after him.

CHAPTER TWENTY-EIGHT

YES, McCrorie truly hated this place.

It was the air. Not just the smell—which was bad enough—but the feeling of it. It was thick. Tasted nasty. Every breath felt like ingesting mildew, mold, and... and... who knows.

He was back at the abandoned dairy processing plant.

This time, he moved through the crumbling hallways, past rusted vats and broken conveyor belts, going deeper into the structure than he had so far. His footsteps echoed off the decaying walls.

He expected to hear the man from the shadows—yelling or screaming or banging on the walls. Maybe even crying. But this time, there was nothing but silence.

This seemed like a bad omen. Especially given what was about to happen.

After all this time working with the Cashman, always by phone, he would finally see the man face-to-face.

His pulse kicked up. Even in this rotten place. Even smelling this rotten air.

He was used to bad air.

The night of the fire, it had been thick and acrid—burning hay and oil and everything else his father had ever beaten into him. He remembered how the flames swallowed the barn, how they devoured the wooden beams, how the heat blistered his arm before he even realized he was burning.

He hadn't meant to burn the barn to the ground.

His father had humiliated him in front of half the town at the auction yard, called him useless and made sure everyone heard it.

McCrorie had wanted his mother so badly that day. Needed her. But she'd been gone two entire years by then.

That night, after another worthless dinner, another round of ridicule, another beating, McCrorie had walked outside with shaking hands and a jaw clenched so tightly it hurt.

He'd only meant to burn some hay.

Not the entire barn.

Not his father.

Not his arms.

Another turn around another corner, and the office lay ahead. McCrorie gasped as he stepped through the doorway.

Submachine guns.

Two armed men flanked a rotting desk, their eyes hard and watchful. And there, in a decrepit chair behind the desk, sat a figure staring through the half-boarded-up-half-shattered-glass window, his back turned to the doorway. Light filtered in, illuminating dust particles that danced languidly in the air.

"Hello, Cashman," McCrorie said.

The figure didn't turn around. Didn't even acknowledge McCrorie's presence.

"I had a couple of my guys tail them after they left the hotel," McCrorie continued, fighting disappointment. "Looks like Joanne Daley had her, um... private eye Clay rough up the guys at the storage facility."

The Cashman's voice was deep, measured. "He's no private eye, and you know it."

"Yes..." McCrorie agreed quietly.

"He's some sort of professional. And he's clearly capable."

"Then how do you want me to proceed?"

"Change the approach. Shift focus to the other person of interest."

McCrorie's brows rose slightly. "You mean—"

"Yes. Him."

McCrorie considered this, then nodded. "I'll handle it."

"I hope so. For your sake, Mr. McCrorie. You do remember the little demonstration we offered you when you agreed to contract for Obsidian?"

A memory slammed into McCrorie.

That night a few weeks ago. Right there at the abandoned dairy facility. The air had been thick with rot, just like now, the walls sweating with decay. Obsidian operatives—large men in dark clothing—had led him into the depths of the plant. Past rusted vats. Over corroded catwalks. Until they reached a room that reeked of blood and bleach.

The man had already been there. Stripped. Bound. Trembling.

What followed was slow. Methodical. The kind of thing that etches itself into a man's mind and never leaves.

McCrorie hadn't seen much; he'd closed his eyes even when the Obsidian men commanded him not to, punching his stomach. He couldn't have forced his eyes open if he wanted to.

But the sounds had been enough.

The wet, sticky peeling. The hoarse, broken shrieks that dissolved into shuddering gasps.

McCrorie hadn't eaten for three days after that.

And he never once thought about crossing Obsidian.

Now, standing in the present, he clenched his jaw. "Yeah. I remember. I'll handle this. You have my word."

He stared at the back of the Cashman's head, willing him to turn around. But the figure remained motionless, silhouetted against the filtered light.

McCrorie had never seen the Cashman's face.

And it looked like he wasn't going to this time, either.

CHAPTER TWENTY-NINE

As the Cadillac roared through the trees, Joanne sat in the passenger seat, eyes glued to her cellular phone's multiplex screen. Anxiety churned in her stomach as she typed in Tracy's number and hit dial.

Clay shot a glance in her direction, assessing the situation, as he kept the car barreling ahead, trees whipping past.

The call rang.

And rang.

And rang...

Then, "What, Mom?" Tracy's irritated voice. "I told you I'm done talking to you."

"Tracy, listen—"

"Save it!" Tracy snapped. "I already helped you. I got you the meaning of *GENEVA*. I'm done here."

"No! That's not—" Joanne stopped herself. Frustration and urgency spiked inside her. That wouldn't do. Not at all. She took a breath, forced her voice steady. "Tracy, where are you?"

A beat of silence. "Back at the hotel. In the suite."

Joanne exhaled. Relief, short-lived.

"I'm about to book my flight back to Seattle," Tracy continued.

Joanne closed her eyes briefly. *She's leaving.* The moment they were getting close, Tracy was slipping away again.

But that wasn't the fight right now.

Definitely not.

"You and Arlo Ford are in danger."

A puzzled pause. "What the hell are you talking about?"

"People are coming for you, Tracy. You need to leave."

Joanne waited. The quiet on the line stretched, and for a moment, she thought Tracy might have hung up.

Finally, Tracy said, "Oh, no..."

Joanne's chest clenched. "I know, I'm sorry to call like this, but—"

"No!" Tracy cut her off, her voice suddenly hushed and taut. "I mean, you're right. *Someone's here!* Right now."

Joanne's heart stopped. "What? Who?"

A rustling sound, movement. "I don't..." Tracy trailed off.

"Tracy, talk to me. What's happening?"

"I just looked out the suite door. There's someone in the hallway. A man. Coming this way. Looking right at me."

Joanne sat bolt upright. "Tracy, listen to me. You need to get out. Now."

A pause. Long. Finally, "I gotta go."

"Tracy, you—"

The line went dead.

Joanne stared at her phone, heart pounding.

Clay didn't need to ask what had happened.

His foot pressed harder on the accelerator, and the Cadillac surged forward.

CHAPTER THIRTY

Tracy stood frozen in the doorway of the hotel suite, the door propped open against her hip, cellular phone still in her hand after having just hung up on Mom.

Her breaths came fast, shallow. Her pulse pounded in her ears.

Because a man was approaching from the end of the hallway outside, and it had only taken Tracy one look at the guy to realize he was a threat.

Large. Muscular physique. Dark clothing—black cargo pants and a tight V-neck shirt.

Another calming breath.

Then, slowly, Tracy leaned out, peering around the doorframe into the hallway.

There he was again.

He was closer now, coming down the hall with purpose. Not running. But not just walking, either.

He was moving with a predator's gait—controlled, efficient. His eyes locked onto her.

No doubt about it. He was coming for her.

Shit.

Tracy turned on her heel, striding down the hall in the opposite direction. At first, she forced herself to keep the pace steady—casual but quick.

That lasted three steps.

Screw it.

She broke into a run.

Behind her, boots pounded against the carpet.

She skidded around the corner hard, nearly colliding with a housekeeping cart. The maid yelped, stumbling back.

"Sorry!" Tracy called over her shoulder.

She didn't slow down.

At the next hallway, she took another sharp turn.

Dammit, Mom!

If Joanne hadn't insisted on the top-floor suite, Tracy might already be outside. Instead, she was stuck in a maze of hallways five stories up.

Her legs burned, the old injury screaming at her.

Not now.

She needed to move.

Because the footsteps were still coming up fast behind her.

She burst through a staff-only door, entering a dim service corridor. A flickering light overhead cast jerky shadows on beige walls.

The exit sign loomed at the end.

She hit the push bar hard, shoving into the stairwell...

...then instantly pivoted, dodging left instead of heading down.

Misdirection.

She took the second exit, popping out into another hall. Kept moving. To a different exit sign.

Pain shot through her shoulder and down into her thighs —throwing gasoline on the fire of her old injury—as she slammed into another push bar, whacking the steel door into the wall.

She flew down the stairs, feet pounding, nearly tripping. Her footsteps hammered through the cinderblock tunnel, sharp and loud, up and down its height.

But as far as she could tell, there was only one set of footsteps—no one was following.

Four floors down, and then she hit the lobby at a dead sprint. Guests turned. A couple near the front desk gawked. The concierge started to speak but shut up when he saw her expression.

Tracy didn't stop.

Through the automatic doors.

Out into the warm Wisconsin air.

Now she allowed herself to slow for a moment, sucked in a deep breath, ready to make a break for the sidewalk...

...and then she saw him.

The same man.

He had just come out of a side exit.

For a moment, he looked around. Scanning.

Then his gaze landed on her.

Tracy's stomach plummeted. She took off again.

Her old instincts kicked in. Rhythm. Breathing. Efficiency.

She had been a star athlete in high school—both track and cross-country. She'd even done two years of college-level cross-country before life got in the way.

But that was a long time ago.

And her body reminded her.

The injury—compartment syndrome.

It had started after the accident in Seattle. A nasty spill on a bike. Deep bruising. Muscle damage.

For years now, it only took a few minutes of running

before the former athlete's legs locked up. Tight, unrelenting. Every time.

It was happening now.

Her muscles felt like lead, and her calves were near implosion.

But she kept running.

A low chainlink fence appeared ahead.

She vaulted it without breaking stride, landing hard, her calves barking in protest. She stumbled, cursing under her breath, but forced herself forward.

A park sign flashed past.

TRAIL SYSTEM – PLYMOUTH RECREATION PARK

Perfect.

She'd never been one for trail running despite being an elite runner who'd spent her life in California and Washington—states filled to the brim with world-class trails.

Now was about the most ideal time to start a trail-running habit.

She darted into the woods, her breath ragged, forcing herself to ignore the sharp ache in her legs. The trail narrowed, winding through low-hanging branches. The air was damp with the scent of leaves and damp earth.

She risked a glance over her shoulder.

The man was still coming, with her now in the trees. And he was gaining.

Panic surged, but Tracy shoved it down.

The trail forked ahead. She took the left path, her feet skidding slightly on loose dirt.

Behind her, she heard a crash. A curse.

The man had misjudged the footing. Fallen.

Tracy pushed harder, pushed through the pain in her calves, which was becoming almost unbearable.

Up ahead, she spotted a fallen tree spanning the path.

Without thinking, she vaulted over it like she had the fence, like the hundreds of hurdles back in high school.

The trail twisted again, winding deeper into the woods. She zigzagged through the trees, using every bit of cover she could find.

Her lungs burned. Her calves screamed. She could feel her entire body giving out.

The trees thinned. Ahead was a shallow ravine.

She slid down, her shoes digging into the dirt, kicking up a cloud of dust. Her legs nearly buckled, but she pressed herself against the embankment.

Chest heaving.

Trying to quiet her breathing.

Footsteps slowed behind her.

And paused.

Tracy bit her lip.

The man cursed, moving past her hiding spot, his boots crunching over the trail above.

Tracy remained perfectly still. Her pulse hammered.

The forest went quiet.

She waited, her back pressed into the cool dirt, legs trembling.

When she was sure the man was gone, she allowed herself to sink back against the embankment.

And exhaled.

CHAPTER THIRTY-ONE

The Cadillac shot down Bluewater Lane, threading through the light traffic, eliciting a few angry horns. Silence kept his gaze steady, mentally following the path he'd taken earlier in the day.

Almost there.

He took a sharp left, screeching within a foot of a slow-moving van, then swiftly veered right onto a side street, the tires squealing in protest.

Joanne sat in the passenger seat with a death grip on the door's pull handle. Her blue eyes were open wide. For a split second, Silence considered her age, considered not scaring her into a heart attack. Then he pushed the thought aside.

Tires squealing, the Cadillac rounded the last corner, and the tidy old rental house appeared. Silence barely braked before throwing the car into park.

"Stay here!" he barked.

This time, Joanne didn't argue. She remained in her seat.

Silence sprinted to the door, retracing his earlier path over the paving stones.

He pounded twice. The door didn't swing open like it had that morning.

"Arlo!"

No response.

He hammered again, harder.

Still nothing.

Silence stepped back and kicked. The door let out a loud, hollow creak as the force of Silence's blow shattered its frame, sending shards of wood flying and clattering to the floor. As it banged open, a figure charged out of the dim interior.

Big Mark.

Protecting his property.

Of course.

His dark eyes were wide, manic. And he was swinging a toilet plunger like a battle axe.

Silence barely dodged. The rubber end slapped against the doorframe with a *thwock*.

He grabbed the man's wrist, pinning the plunger to the wall. Big Mark went for a swing with the other arm, but Silence caught that wrist, too, and pretzeled him up. The plunger dropped.

"Easy," Silence said, swallowed. "Not here to hurt you."

Big Mark thrashed for a second, then sagged. Silence let go.

"Sorry, *amigo*. I thought you were one of them."

"Arlo," Silence said. "Where is he?"

"Arlo's gone. Those same men from last night, they come, they grab him."

Silence surveyed the rental house. Nothing was amiss. No upended furniture, no strewn belongings, no cracked drywall.

Whoever had taken Arlo acted quickly, carefully, leaving no evidence behind. Professionals.

Obsidian.

His shoulders tensed.

"When?" he said.

Big Mark shook his head. "An hour ago."

He remembered what the big guy in the denim shirt had said out in the trees—that Arlo was to be the bait to draw out Layne Grosicki.

With Layne dead, they must have taken Arlo as bait to draw out someone else.

And that "someone" was surely Silence.

Obsidian knew Silence was closing in.

Silence motioned toward the shattered door frame. "Sorry. Will pay for it." He swallowed. "Leave this place. It's unsafe."

Silence returned to the Cadillac, where Joanne waited.

He told her what happened and put the car into gear.

Joanne placed a hand on her cheek. "I still can't reach Tracy on her mobile phone," she said, her voice unsteady. "Now what? Arlo and... and Tracy. Both taken. *Now what?*"

Her tone rose with each word, climbing toward hysteria.

As he merged onto the highway and gunned the accelerator, Silence considered her question for a moment. "Now I do..." He swallowed. "What I do best."

CHAPTER THIRTY-TWO

SOMEHOW, Caruso's tiny office felt even more cramped than before, like the walls of files were closing in, ready to devour.

Along with Joanne, Silence was back in the pair of chairs facing the food inspector's temporary Plymouth desk, with Caruso on the other side. Silence and Caruso were watching Joanne, who was using her cellular phone, hunched over, her voice low.

As Joanne ended the call, she turned. Her expression shifted from intense focus to immense relief.

"Tracy's safe," she said with a touch of disbelief, like she hadn't dared to hope for good news. "She made it to a cheap motel. Paid with cash."

Silence nodded.

Shrewd. Intelligent.

He was beginning to like this Tracy.

"Safest place..." he said and swallowed. "For her right now."

Joanne exhaled. The tension she'd been holding onto all day seemed to loosen. But Silence could still see something in her posture. A tightness that hadn't eased.

She wasn't just relieved. She was thinking.

Hard.

A mother's worry...

Caruso shook his head. "You two are causing me a hell of a headache. But fine." He reached into a locked file cabinet, pulled out a stack of paper, and slid it across the desk.

"These are Layne's notes," Caruso said. "I guess you've earned a look."

That's why Silence had come—to get Layne's notes from Caruso, intel that had become a Holy Grail, one that might hold the final clues.

Silence took them from Caruso.

Finally.

The stack was thin. Only a few sheets of computer-printed paper.

But before he could start reading, Joanne spoke. "Before we get into this... there's something I need to say."

Silence looked up. Waited.

Joanne's fingers twisted in her lap, tracing the letters branded into her journal's leather cover. She was clearly working up to something.

"It's about Tracy," she said. "Why she doesn't want anything to do with me."

She hesitated. Then pushed forward.

"I was cruel." Joanne's voice was raw. "Not just to Tracy. To a lot of people. Students. Like I told you about last night. I see that now. I was a bully. But I didn't think I was. I thought I was 'toughening people up.'"

Silence didn't move. He just listened.

"Tracy wanted to be a photographer," Joanne continued. "I thought it was foolish. A dead end. I told her that. Repeatedly. And then... I did something worse."

She swallowed. Looked away.

"She got her first big break. A magazine gig in Sacramento. She was thrilled. Didn't tell me about it at first. I found out on my own, and I... I called the editor. Behind her back. Told them not to hire her. Said she was unreliable."

Silence's jaw tightened.

Damn. She really is *a bitch.*

"When Tracy found out... that was it. She cut me off. Got the job in spite of my meddling. Moved to Sacramento first. Then, after her divorce, to Seattle, even farther away. I think she just wanted to be as far from me as possible."

Silence had no doubt that was true.

Joanne sighed, ran a hand through her silver hair. "She had every reason to leave. Every reason to hate me."

She glanced at the files in Silence's hands.

"Just like Layne did." Joanne looked at him, her voice quieter now. She clutched her journal tighter. "I can't take any of it back. But I can try to do better."

Joanne looked down and back up, this time at Caruso, who had an uncomfortably awkward look on his face.

"Sorry," Joanne said to him.

Caruso nodded.

Silence didn't console Joanne, didn't say *That was a long time ago* or *It's not that bad*.

Because it *was* that bad.

And Joanne knew it.

So, instead of acknowledging the confession, he moved to something more important.

The mission.

He looked at Layne's notes.

The text was sparse but dense, written in shorthand and broken sentences.

But Silence was accustomed to broken English.

A narrative emerged—a tangled web of connections Layne had uncovered.

Rud's shipping manifests and those of a handful of other

Plymouth cheese shops—every single one tied back to Julian McCrorie. Several of the shipments were stopped at the port due to contamination. That's what had tipped Layne off in the first place.

Then Silence saw the dates...

Joanne must have seen his reaction because she leaned in and said, "What is it?"

Silence's jaw tightened. "If Layne's dates are correct..." He flipped through the pages, confirming. "...then Obsidian is in town now."

Joanne's face changed. A memory clicking into place.

"Yes!" she said, eyes widening. "The guy at the shack in the woods said the shipment was being moved tonight! Remember?"

She was right.

Silence exhaled. There was one conclusion to draw from all of this: they were out of time.

Obsidian was active. Right now. Ready to move a shipment of biological weaponry out of Plymouth tonight.

Layne Grosicki had stumbled onto something massive before he died. And Obsidian was about to execute the final phase.

Silence turned on Joanne. "We gotta go. Now." He swallowed. "If—"

His cellular phone rang.

Silence pulled it from his pocket. The multiplex displayed a familiar number.

Harvey.

He flipped the phone open. "Yes?"

A pause. Then Harvey's voice, sheepish, almost ashamed.

"Hey-a, Clay. You know how you told me I shouldn't help out that kid at the pawnshop?"

Silence straightened in his chair, instincts flaring.

Oh, shit...

"Yes...?"

"Well, I did. His name's Jesse. And..." Harvey trailed off, voice tight. "Look, I didn't think it'd be a big deal, but..." He trailed off again. Then, suddenly, "5028 Ashen Wharf Road! I'm at 5028—"

A sudden scuffle on the other end of the line.

A muffled shout.

The phone clattered.

A gruff voice barked something unintelligible.

"Harvey?" Silence said. "*Harvey!*"

Then nothing.

The line went dead.

Silence stared at the phone in his hand, adrenaline surging.

Joanne put her hand on Silence's shoulder. "What happened?"

Silence didn't answer. He was already on his feet, heading for the door.

CHAPTER THIRTY-THREE

TRACY SAT on the edge of the bed in a room that smelled like stale smoke, industrial cleaner, and something sour lurking beneath it all.

The motel was the kind of place where the carpet was sticky in some spots, the floral comforter was stiff with age, and the walls had absorbed decades of cigarette smoke, leaving a yellowish film behind.

It was a jarring switch from the luxury of the suite across town, with its plush carpets and crisp white linens. That place had smelled of citrus and money. Here, the air conditioner rattled, the bathroom light flickered, and something brown stained the ceiling.

She had her Macintosh laptop set up on the rickety desk, plugged into the motel's phone port. The AOL screen glowed blue and white, and the modem had begun its screeching, warbling song—the digital handshake of the 1990s, the sound of stepping into the Internet.

She drummed her fingers against the desk as she waited. The connection process was sluggish. Usually, she had the patience for it. But now, with everything at stake, it was excruciating.

Tracy's fingers hovered over the trackball, hesitating. This was the right thing to do—she knew that. Mom and Clay needed her help, and the stakes were too high to let personal history get in the way.

And yet... her hand trembled slightly at the idea of assisting Mom again after all that had happened between them.

The modem screeched again, another step in the connection process. Almost there.

Tracy closed her eyes briefly, letting out a slow breath. The memory still stung, even after all this time. The anger and betrayal she'd felt when Joanne called her first big client —without her knowledge or permission—and tried to convince them not to work with her.

Mom's controlling tendencies had always been a source of tension, but that moment had been the breaking point. Tracy had worked so hard to establish herself as a photographer, to build a career that reflected her independence and creativity. She'd finally begun to carve out a life on her own terms, only for Joanne to undermine it with a single phone call.

That wasn't the only thing, of course. Joanne's constant belittling of Tracy's dreams—her dismissive remarks about photography being a "dead-end pursuit"—had left deep scars long before the client debacle. Tracy had tried to move on, to bury the resentment and focus on building a new life far away from her mother.

But here she was, pulled back into Joanne Daley's orbit, the wounds reopening as they worked together to unravel the mystery of Layne Grosicki's death.

Layne.

His name stirred a different kind of ache—nostalgia and

regret. Tracy and Layne had been inseparable as kids in the quiet streets of Morro Bay. He'd been her confidant, her partner in wholesome mischief. But as their lives diverged, that bond had frayed, reduced to occasional updates and Christmas cards.

And then, somewhere along the line, he was just gone.

Now, he was dead.

The modem let out a final triumphant screech, and the AOL screen loaded fully, filling the dim motel room with its glow. Tracy opened her eyes, refocusing on the task at hand.

Mom and Clay needed help finding Arlo Ford. Tracy didn't know Arlo, had never met the kid. But that didn't matter. He needed help.

And he cared about Layne.

If helping Mom was the only way to honor Layne's memory and protect Arlo, so be it.

With a final exhale, Tracy clicked on the AOL homepage, then navigated to the message boards, ready to start pulling information.

CHAPTER THIRTY-FOUR

ALONE IN HIS aging Dodge Ram pickup, McCrorie thought he had a moment of rest, a moment to decompress.

The interior smelled of dirt, old coffee, and a faint trace of motor oil. The cracked vinyl seats had molded to his shape over the years, and the dashboard was faded from too many summers baking in the sun.

The low rumble of the engine. The rhythmic click of the vents. It all wrapped around him like an old jacket, taking him away from his recent troubles.

And then his cellular phone rang.

He looked at the number on the multiplex. Hesitated. And flipped the phone open.

"Yes, Cashman?"

There was an immediate response. "Your man's incompetence allowed Tracy Simmons to escape."

McCrorie's jaw tightened. "I... I've seen to the man in question. It won't happen again."

A scoffing breath crackled through the line. "After this mess, McCrorie, your words don't mean much anymore. Maybe you're not worth keeping around."

McCrorie stiffened, face flushing.

His skin flushed, too—with perspiration—at the mere thought of what the man on the other end of the line could do to him.

That memory flashed through McCrorie's mind again.

When he'd been forced to watch the Obsidian operatives skin a man alive.

That individual had been McCrorie's predecessor...

McCrorie swallowed. "I swear to you, I'll—"

"Shut up. Words are cheap. Joanne Daley and the professional are leaving the business park now. Take care of them."

"You mean—"

Beep.

The Cashman was gone.

The business park...

He had to think for a moment. That was way on the other side of town on Wisconsin-23.

Shit!

He stomped the gas pedal.

McCrorie barely made it.

He spotted the silver Cadillac rolling toward the exit, picking up speed. No time to chase it down on the highway. He needed to cut them off here.

He slammed the gas. The Ram roared forward, tires screeching across the massive parking lot. He veered hard, skidding between rows of parked cars, then straightened out—barreling directly toward the Cadillac's path.

At the last second, the Cadillac braked hard, tires screaming. McCrorie stomped his own brakes, swinging the truck broadside, blocking their escape.

For a beat, everything froze.

Through the windshield, he saw Joanne Daley in the passenger set, wide-eyed, bracing herself against the dash. But the professional, Clay, was unphased.

He just stared.

At McCrorie.

A silent standoff.

Then, the Cadillac's door kicked open. A massive figure stepped out.

McCrorie felt the rush—adrenaline, satisfaction. This was the man who had wasted time, money, resources.

McCrorie shoved open his own door and stepped out in one smooth motion. His jacket shifted just enough to reveal the dull gleam of his Beretta's barrel.

"Well, someone's sure in a hurry," he called out. "I'm sorry, did I cut you off?"

The professional didn't flinch. "Piss off."

McCrorie faltered for a half-second.

Holy shit...

The man's voice was... wrong. Not just rough but unnatural.

Composing himself, McCrorie grinned, all teeth. "Just a friendly chat, man to man."

He held the professional's stare. The guy stood relaxed, weight balanced on the balls of his feet—a fighter's stance.

Behind him, Daley stayed frozen in the passenger seat.

McCrorie felt a muscle in his jaw twitch. The professional wasn't trying to avoid a fight. He was preparing for one.

McCrorie's hand inched toward his Beretta. The professional clenched his fists, forearms going taut.

Behind them, Daley shifted, uncertain.

McCrorie couldn't back down.

Obsidian will skin you alive, he reminded himself.

No, he wouldn't back down.

He stepped forward.

CHAPTER THIRTY-FIVE

Silence knew who this man must be.

The guy was in his forties. Red hair, faded and thinning beneath a greasy ball cap. Pale freckles scattered across his face and arms. His face was hard-edged, his nose crooked from an old break. Pale blue eyes, close-set. But what caught Silence's attention first—what made him pause—was the man's arms.

From wrist to shoulder, thick, uneven scar tissue wrapped his limbs in a wicked sheath. Burn scars. Old and deep. Silence recognized that kind of injury, the way the skin never quite settled right, the way the texture shifted under the light.

After reading Layne's notes, there was no confusion—this man was Julian McCrorie. The scarred man. The man Layne had been trying to track down.

For a moment, a strange sort of kinship twisted through Silence. The man before him wore his scars on the outside. Silence carried his inside—a throat ruined, a voice forever fractured.

But this wasn't a moment for reflection.

McCrorie's hand was already twitching toward his gun.

Silence had spotted it immediately. A Beretta 92F, nearly identical to Silence's Beretta 92FS.

Silence's own Beretta was holstered, half-hidden beneath his jacket, also itching to be drawn. But not here. Not with people still coming and going, filing out of the office building, all briefcases and sensible heels.

Then McCrorie moved.

He drew his Beretta and lunged forward like a coiled spring unfurling, holding the pistol high in his right hand, trying to force an opening.

Silence didn't bite. He let his mind merge with the moment—a mindfulness technique C.C. had taught him—and time stretched out as McCrorie closed the gap.

McCrorie threw a hook—clumsy, unbalanced. Silence tilted his head just enough to let it skim past, then snapped forward, grabbing the man's wrist.

McCrorie snarled, twisting against the grip, but Silence had already stepped in, locking the arm, pressing against the stiffened limb.

A strangled yelp from McCrorie as his arm contorted. He dropped to one knee. His Beretta clattered onto the pavement.

McCrorie thrashed, breaking free in a violent shake, then barreled forward in a brutish tackle.

Silence allowed it.

He rode the momentum, arched back, then lashed out—a roundhouse kick. The *mawashi geri* cracked against McCrorie's hip. The impact echoed through the parking lot.

Shock flickered in McCrorie's eyes briefly before a grimace twisted his face. He stumbled, shoved himself upright, retreated just enough to breathe.

But Silence didn't allow him to breathe. Silence attacked.

A single stride. A backhand swing.

Out of nowhere, a small child darted between two parked cars, giggling, oblivious to the fight unfolding before her.

Behind her, a woman lunged forward, reaching desperately. "Emily, stop!"

Silence's attention snapped to them for a split second—

And McCrorie seized the opening.

He drove his shoulder into Silence's solar plexus. The air rushed from Silence's lungs as McCrorie followed with a brutal uppercut that caught Silence square on the chin.

Stars exploded across Silence's vision. He staggered back.

In the second it took Silence's head to clear, McCrorie was already back in his truck. The engine roared to life, tires squealing. He barreled out of the parking lot.

Minutes later, Silence brought the Cadillac to a screeching halt at the curb in front of a rundown stretch of low-budget motels on the outskirts of Plymouth. A small faded sign beneath the main sign read *Rooms By The Hour*, telling Silence everything he needed to know about the place.

His eyes found the window of room 121, Tracy's room, and through the sheer curtain, he spotted a barely visible figure at a desk, typing on a laptop.

He didn't even take the Cadillac out of park—had to get to Harvey, had to hurry!—just whipped around to Joanne in the passenger seat.

5028 Ashen Wharf Road.

The address had shouted out before the phone call was cut off. It kept playing in Silence's mind like a drumbeat.

5028 Ashen Wharf Road.

5028 Ashen Wharf Road.

"Get inside. Stay with..." he said and swallowed. "Tracy. I have to..." Another swallow. "Get to Harvey."

Joanne looked out the passenger window and remained frozen. Silence's fingers tightened on the steering wheel, but he gave her a moment. Just a moment.

"I see her in there," Joanne said, still looking out the window.

Silence looked over her shoulder and saw her too—Tracy, hunched over the laptop in the dim motel room.

"Other than that phone call, we haven't spoken in years," Joanne continued. She turned and looked at Silence. "I'm... lost, Clay. I don't know what to do."

More frustration flushed over Silence. He needed to get to Harvey. He didn't have time to be a cheerleader for a woman who, by all accounts, had been a complete asshole for most of her adult life.

So Silence didn't respond.

As Joanne exhaled heavily and fumbled open the door, C.C. spoke up.

Love, she said. *Come on.*

It was all she needed to say.

He called out to Joanne. "Hey."

Joanne was halfway out the door. She turned around and stooped over to look back at Silence.

"I hope..." Silence said, swallowed. "It goes well."

Joanne gave a weak smile. "Thank you." She shut the door.

And Silence reminded himself of Harvey's panicked voice, the phone call playing in his head again.

He peeled off.

CHAPTER THIRTY-SIX

THE WINDING ROAD blurred past in a mosaic of concrete and streetlights, the storefronts and intersections of Plymouth streaking by as Silence pushed the Cadillac to its limits. The engine growled.

5028 Ashen Wharf Road...

Get there!

5028 Ashen Wharf Road!

Silence took a deep, diaphragmatic breath—a calming technique C.C. had taught him.

Any moment now, he'd arrive. He had little idea what to expect. Other than violence. That part was a given.

He needed to be ready.

His phone trilled from the center console, the ringtone cutting through the thrum of the Cadillac's acceleration. A glance at the multiplex showed a Watchers number.

Falcon.

Silence's Prefect. His boss.

The man whose directive Silence frequently disregarded: *No involvement in local matters.*

Of course Falcon was calling right now.

Shit.

Silence flipped open the phone, keeping one hand on the wheel. "Sir?"

Falcon's voice came sharp but not in full condemnation mode. Not yet, anyway. "Suppressor, you've been good about staying out of local affairs so far during this mission... but what are you up to now?"

Silence's grip tightened on the wheel.

He knew what was happening here. It was that damn dot in his arm. The Watchers could track his every move, his every deviation from their script. He was host to a GPS dot —surgically embedded, hidden under a small strip of scar tissue on his right forearm. It was a permanent part of him, a monitoring device.

The Watchers were always watching him.

The line remained silent. Falcon wanted an answer.

"Following up..." Silence said finally. He swallowed. "On something."

"I see. So nothing important, then?"

"No."

That... was a lie. Silence hated to do it, but sometimes it needed to be done.

"Really?" Falcon said, clearly not buying it. "Because I see you're barreling through Plymouth, and if I had to guess, you're headed for this abandoned warehouse. 5028 Ashen Wharf Road, is that it?"

Falcon was clearly staring at a digital map, watching a few blinking pixels that represented Silence as he tore through Plymouth's streets.

Silence didn't respond.

"Mm-hmm," Falcon said. "As I look it up on the ol' system here, I see this warehouse has connections to gang activity."

Gang activity?! Shit!

"But I see absolutely nothing," Falcon continued, "that

would tie it to the Layne Grosicki matter, nor any mentions of it in your status updates."

Silence didn't respond.

There was a hiss on the line as Falcon let out a sigh. "Dammit, Suppressor. No involvement in local matters. Remember that. I'm watching you."

"Yes, sir."

Beep.

Falcon was gone.

Silence snapped the phone shut, shoving it into his pocket. He hated being monitored. It left a lingering, nasty aftertaste. No matter where he went, no matter how careful he was, they were always watching.

That damn GPS dot in his arm.

But he couldn't dwell on it.

He needed to get to Harvey.

The Cadillac slid to a stop, tires skidding over cracked pavement. The streets were dark, lined with hollowed-out industrial buildings, long abandoned. Everything was gray, dead.

Silence killed the engine. Stepped out. His boots crunched on loose gravel.

He scanned the area, took in the hulking warehouse ahead, a shadow against the dying sky, which was dark pink streaked with purple clouds.

5028 Ashen Wharf Road.

It loomed like a forgotten relic, its corrugated metal siding scarred with rust, streaked with grime.

The call from Harvey still echoed in his mind: *You know how you told me I shouldn't help out that kid at the pawnshop?*

And then the sound of a struggle.

Silence sprinted off, slipping into the shadows, approaching the warehouse's side entrance. The door hung ajar, rusted hinges groaning in the breeze. He cleared the threshold, moved inside.

The air was moist and rotten. Pale light spilled through gaps in the walls. Silence's eyes adjusted.

And saw movement. In the back corner.

The "struggle" he'd heard was a pair of junkies shooting up. One on the ground, the other propped against the wall. They looked in Silence's direction and laughed.

Silence scanned the space for any sign of Harvey or his captors.

Nothing.

Aside from the junkies and some scattered debris, the warehouse was empty.

A rare sensation twisted in Silence's stomach. Helplessness. A gut-wrenching disappointment he hadn't felt in a long time.

Silence didn't deal in uncertainties—he made things happen, he forced the world to align.

But now...

...Harvey was gone.

And he had no idea where.

Frustration came in, too, swirling around with the desperation—because he realized what he had to do.

He pulled out his phone. Flipped it open. Pressed and held the 2 button—speed dial.

An immediate response. Another random Specialist. This time, it was a male voice. "Specialist."

Silence proceeded with protocol. "Suppressor, A-23."

"Confirmed. State your business."

"Information retrieval."

There was the sound of keyboard typing, a pause, then,

"You've been making a lot of those this assignment." A bit of cautious skepticism in the Specialist's tone.

Yes, Plymouth had been a particularly information-heavy assignment. Which made this off-mission information retrieval request all the more likely to get red-flagged.

Especially since that bastard Falcon had just called, hounding him.

"Yes, sir," Silence said, swallowed. "Gang activity." Swallow. "In Plymouth, Wisconsin."

"Wait a minute..."

Silence's heart rate went up a tick, expecting a closed door, expecting to be shut down in his effort to find Harvey.

"You're flagged in the system. We were just about to call you. Further details on Obsidian. Since you alerted us to their presence in Wisconsin, a Specialist did some further digging. Seems they have an eye on the UN Peacekeeping Gala in New York."

"Sir?"

"I know, I know. It's not Obsidian's style to hit such a high-profile target at such a public event. But their real focus isn't the crowd—it's one man: Under-Secretary Matthias Renaud, the UN's top official overseeing global counterterrorism efforts. He's been a relentless force against their operations, spearheading international crackdowns on their networks, freezing assets, and coordinating elite task forces to dismantle their infrastructure.

Renaud loves cheese. His notorious quirk. The guy's a well-known foodie, borderline obsessive about rare and artisanal cheeses from around the world. He's even talked about it in TV interviews. That's why Obsidian is using it to get to him—at the hors d'oeuvres table. The other attendees who eat the cheese—the diplomats, the military leaders—are just collateral damage. Renaud is the target."

Now Silence's heart rate went even higher.

"When is..." he said, swallowed. "Summit?"

"Next week."

Next week...

...and the shipment of Obsidian's tainted cheese was being moved *that night*.

"Anyway, something to be aware of," the Specialist said. "You were wanting to know about gang activity in Plymouth."

"Yes, sir."

"One moment." Ten seconds later, "The only true gang activity in Plymouth seems to be the occasional infiltration from a Milwaukee gang called Los Cráneos Huecos." The Specialist's tone shifted, becoming grimmer. "Translates to 'The Hollow Skulls.' They started in Milwaukee's South Side back in the seventies. Originally neighborhood protection, if you can believe it. Now they're one of the most vicious outfits in the Midwest."

Vicious.

Silence's mind flashed on Harvey. Guileless, awkward Harvey with his trivia and his triangles and his beloved air plant.

"How so?" Silence said.

"Their signature move is skull-crushing." A pause. "Literal skull-crushing. Bats, sledgehammers. Bodies turn up in Lake Michigan, faces unrecognizable. It's their calling card."

Harvey...

Silence absorbed this. "Leadership?"

"Run by a real charmer named Mateo Vargas. Street name 'El Gordo.' Big guy, late thirties, covered in tattoos. Has their hollow skull symbol on his right forearm. Look for the white tank top and gold skull pendant. Seems that's about all he ever wears, his go-to outfit."

"Operations?"

"Everything dirty you can think of. Meth, heroin, loan-sharking. They target low-income folks with predatory loans, then use extreme violence for collection. We're talking arson, family member assaults, public executions. They've also got their fingers in human trafficking."

"Colors?"

"Gray and black. Members wear gray bandanas, hoodies. Their symbol—that hollow skull—shows up as graffiti where they're active. It's a warning sign."

"Understood."

"That's all I've got. Good luck, Suppressor."

Beep.

The call ended. Silence pocketed his phone.

Yes, this move would flag him and alert Falcon and the others that he was deviating from his mission. There would be questions later. Consequences.

But saving Harvey took precedence.

Plus, there was another missing soul—Arlo Ford.

For now, though, there was an even more pressing matter—biological weapons from a major terrorist group being moved through Plymouth.

Tonight.

With the ultimate target being a UN function next week.

Silence ran back to the Cadillac.

CHAPTER THIRTY-SEVEN

THIS WAS CERTAINLY a different set of accommodations than Joanne had grown accustomed to in Plymouth.

She stood in a cramped motel room. Sagging mattress. Patchy carpet. Water-stained ceiling. The air smelled like mildew and cigarettes.

The environment made the moment even more uncomfortable than it already was.

Across from her, Tracy sat at the desk, her back turned, arms crossed tightly over her chest, a laptop computer casting her in a pale glow.

From behind, all Joanne could see was a silhouette. But the mirror to the side revealed a bit more of Tracy.

Straight, chestnut brown hair, tied back in a no-nonsense ponytail. A face that carried traces of both youth and wear. Faint crow's feet at the corners of her blue eyes. Tracy's fair skin, inherited from Joanne's Irish ancestry, seemed even paler under the buzzing fluorescent light overhead. She wore a light sweater over a simple blouse and dark blue slacks.

Plain and simple and pure. Just like she'd always been.

Several long minutes had passed since Joanne had knocked on the door—receiving the briefest of moments of eye contact from Tracy—and entered the space. Tracy had immediately gone back to her computer. Since then, all had been quiet aside from the muffled shouts of some argument in the next room and the hum of an overworked air conditioning unit.

Joanne had tried to breach the divide with a few awkward words.

There'd been no response.

Tracy had just pointed to a notebook, which Joanne had taken, finding her notes from her Internet research, which were scant. After several minutes of trying to piece something together from the notes, Joanne found nothing conclusive. She had called Clay's cellular and reported the lack of development.

Now, for several minutes, she'd been trying to work up the nerve to talk to Tracy again.

Clearing her throat, Joanne tried once more. "Tracy, I ... again, I owe you an explanation. For back then, what I did."

Tracy remained motionless at the desk, revealing nothing. Joanne wet her lips, pressed on.

"I know I said it already, but I have to say it again face-to-face. I'm sorry for hurting you like that. For letting my need to control things get away from me so badly."

She shifted her weight awkwardly, gaze dropping.

"I did try to sabotage your career. I did. But I was trying to protect you, in my own awful way." Her shoulders slumped. "I was wrong. I know that's not close to good enough, but I need you to hear it straight from me."

When the continued quiet stretched unbroken, Joanne risked a hesitant half-step closer.

"I'm working on it now, I swear, being a better person. I

even bought this journal, and... *ugh*... Anyway, I know it doesn't undo what I did. And I'm so sorry."

She swallowed.

"Point is, what happened back then doesn't erase the love I've always had for you, no matter how much I screwed up showing it."

Quiet swept in once more, broken only by the distant hum of traffic outside and the rhythmic buzz of the dying fluorescent light overhead. Joanne shifted her weight between her feet, then exhaled softly.

"I guess that's all I have to say. The apology's long overdue, but you deserve it all the same."

She looked toward the door. The chipped, peeling paint. The rusted chain lock hanging at an awkward angle.

She wondered if she should just leave.

When she turned back around, she found Tracy finally facing her.

Her features were creased with lingering pain, old scars long buried. But she held Joanne's gaze unflinchingly. Stoic.

When she spoke at last, her voice was low and steady. "I believe you're sorry. But trust..." She paused. "Trust isn't easy to rebuild once broken. I can't just pretend it didn't happen."

Just when it looked like Tracy might say something else, *You're forgiven*, perhaps...

Whack!

...the door flew open, flooding the dingy room with harsh light from the flickering vacancy sign outside. Both Joanne and Tracy jumped as Clay barreled inside and came to a sudden stop.

"I've had time to think," Clay said without preamble. He swallowed. "We need to go. Now."

"What? Why?" Joanne said.

Tracy's brow furrowed. "You said we'd be safest here."

Clay's cold eyes cut through the dim light. He took a slow breath.

"I was wrong. They've been watching us," he said and swallowed. "Let's roll."

CHAPTER THIRTY-EIGHT

SHADOWS CLOAKED Rud's Artisanal Cheese Shop's dormant equipment, dimly lit by the fading sunlight filtering through the windows. Silence moved through the space, with Joanne and Tracy trailing behind him, their footsteps echoing as they ventured into the semi-dark.

Silence scanned the shop, alert for any lingering muscle from his last visit.

Finding none, his focus shifted to the papers in his hands—Rud's records that he'd managed to snag on that first incursion—shipping manifests, inventory lists, and email threads with oblique references to "special order items."

There had to be something in the morass to drag Obsidian's true motives into the light.

He hadn't grabbed everything the first time, only what he could carry, what he deemed necessary under a time crunch—the alarm had been blaring after the man on the dirt bike had burst through the front entrance.

It was only during the quick road trip back from Plymouth's outskirts that it dawned on Silence who had been in the position to know everything at all times...

Silence led Joanne and Tracy into Rud's office. At the desk, he spread the papers wide, mixing them with fresh documents yanked from the shelf as he rifled through personnel reports and time cards. Nothing but bit players, useless minutiae, pointless details. He discarded each sheet lacking immediate relevance, slowly winnowing toward potentially critical information.

Then...

Something significant.

A shipping document. The header labeled it simply *OBSIDIAN SHIPMENT.*

A notation in compact script along the margin caught Silence's attention next:

Caruso guarantees this second Obsidian shipment will pass inspection.

Shit...

"Just as I..." Silence said, swallowed. "Thought."

Joanne cocked her head. "What is it?"

Silence pointed at the name on the note and said, "Stuart Caruso."

Joanne gasped, hands going to her mouth.

Tracy said, "Mom, who's that? Who is Stuart Caruso?"

It took Joanne a moment. She lowered her hands. "A food inspector out of Milwaukee. He was following up on Layne's whistleblowing. He was the only person in town who believed me..."

Silence stepped forward. "And he's actually..." he said and swallowed. "Working for Obsidian." Another swallow. "Caruso must be the Cashman."

Silence shuffled to the other side of the desk, pulled Rud's computer monitor closer. His fingers flew across the keys to access the computer's spreadsheets. He pulled up cached records still lingering from Rud's usage despite attempts at erasure, cross-referencing dates and entries between digital artifacts and the paper documents.

"Here!" he said after a moment. "Here is where—"

"Wait," Joanne said, cutting him off. "Clay, look at this."

She was holding a business card that she'd pulled from one of the stacks of paper. It was from a food inspector out of Milwaukee. The name was listed as *STUART CARUSO*.

But the man smiling in the photo looked nothing like the man Silence had known as Stuart Caruso...

In a flash, he put it together.

Despite the pain in his throat, he found himself mumbling the crumbs of his thoughts aloud. "Food inspector... cheese." He swallowed. "Weapons... shipments."

Tracy stepped closer. "Clay, what is it?"

Silence quickly pulled his PenPal from his pocket and scribbled out a note, slapped it on the desk for the women to read.

Obsidian must have gotten wind of Layne poking around Plymouth. When they found out that he had a friendly food inspector willing to listen to his tale and come to Plymouth to investigate, they dispatched the Cashman to intercept Caruso and take his place. The real Caruso would be easy to replace in a town where no one knew his face. As a "food inspector," the Obsidian man was able to ensure this upcoming shipment will make it past inspections.

Joanne and Tracy just stared at the note for a long moment. Finally, Joanne said, "So what do we do now?"

Silence went back to the computer, back to what he was going to show them a few moments earlier before Joanne cut him off. He poked a finger at the monitor.

Joanne squinted at the screen, read what Silence was indicating, and deciphered it out loud. "Rud had frequent meetings with the Cashman at an abandoned dairy plant on the edge of town. That's where they were shipping out his tainted cheese. Donovan Creek Dairy Processing Plant."

"We have a location..." Silence said and swallowed. He then poked a finger at the note.

Ensure shipment readied on time, 2100, the day in question. Absolutely critical this shipment reaches Obsidian reps. (SC)

"...and a time," Silence finished. "9 pm."

Tracy nodded, her eyes bouncing across the computer screen as she read the email Silence had pulled up on the screen, putting all the pieces together.

She said, "The Cashman is going to personally deliver the final batch of weapon-infused cheese to the clients at the abandoned Donovan plant... tonight!"

Silence looked at his watch. "In an hour."

The first step was ensuring the weaponized cheese never reached its intended recipients. Contact the authorities? No, working under the guise of the food inspector Stuart Caruso, the Cashman would have surely made connections over the last week with the Plymouth authorities.

This called for something far less elegant.

Silence was going to cut off the shipment.

He shoved himself away from the computer.

Suddenly, two other ideas materialized, making him angry at himself for forgetting them.

First, Harvey was still out there, somewhere, in danger, location unknown.

Second, there was another person unaccounted for...

He looked at the other two. "We still don't know..." he said and swallowed. "Where to find Arlo." He pointed at the computer. "Dig deep. Find out where he is." Another swallow. "And save him."

He shot out of the chair.

Behind him, Tracy shouted, "But where are you going?"

Silence called out over his shoulder. "To Donovan Creek."

CHAPTER THIRTY-NINE

His name was Alan Pincombe.

But for the last week and a half, he'd been calling himself Stuart Caruso, the name he'd stolen from the food inspector out of Milwaukee.

The man whispering with the other prisoner somewhere deeper in the bowels of the abandoned structure.

Pincombe could hear them. Little voices. Trying to be quiet. Not realizing how far sound carried in the hollow remains of the derelict facility.

This place—the former Donovan Creek Dairy Processing Plant—had become familiar to Pincombe. Comfortable, even. Despite the rot, the stench, the hazards, it suited him.

He walked deeper into the facility, his brogues tapping against the concrete, the sound echoing off the walls. Turning a corner, he found the man he was here to meet—staring back at him, head tilted in confusion.

Julian McCrorie.

This was the man who, for months, had been Pincombe's right-hand man—from a distance. They'd only ever spoken by phone. First, when Pincombe was out of state. Then, for the last week and a half, in Plymouth.

Now, seeing him in person for the first time, Pincombe felt a quiet, crawling disgust.

McCrorie looked exactly like the kind of low-rent thug Pincombe had expected—white-trash filth with dirt under his nails, reeking of cheap cigarettes and motor oil. His faded ball cap barely concealed the thinning, greasy red hair, and his sun-freckled skin had the uneven, weathered texture of a man who'd spent too much time outside and not enough time evolving.

And then there were the scars.

Pincombe's lip curled at the sight of the puckered, grotesque burns twisting up McCrorie's arms, mangled from wrist to shoulder, like something you'd see on a backwoods meth cook who'd gotten sloppy with a propane tank.

Everything about McCrorie reeked of poverty, bad decisions, and the kind of desperation that made a man easy to control.

McCrorie narrowed his eyes. "So you're... the Cashman, huh?"

Pincombe smiled. Kept it subtle. The kind of smile you give a dog before you kick it.

"That' right, Julian." He paused, studying that look of slight remembrance in the other man's eyes. He grinned. "I look familiar to you, don't I?"

McCrorie nodded.

"But you don't know why," Pincombe added.

McCrorie nodded again.

Pincombe snickered. "Because I've only been in town for less than a week. I introduced myself at the diner. As Stuart Caruso."

McCrorie's eyes widened, and he snapped his fingers. "Yes! But—"

"I've been running the show over the phone all these months," McCrorie said. "From Brooklyn. Obsidian never wanted boots on the ground in pissant Plymouth. But then Layne Grosicki started asking questions. Got the Milwaukee food inspector on his side. We saw an opportunity. I got flown in, took Caruso's place, set up a small contingent. We... handled Grosicki. And since then, I've been monitoring you and your work."

McCrorie chewed on this for a moment. Pincombe could see the wheels turning in his head. Slowly. He already knew that McCrorie wasn't the sharpest knife in the drawer, but meeting the guy now in person, McCrorie was even stupider than expected.

Finally, McCrorie's eyes flicked to the side—toward the distant whispers, somewhere deeper in the complex—and said, "So the real Caruso... that's who I've been hearing in this place?"

Pincombe nodded. "Our prisoner. One of our *two* prisoners now." He gestured down the hall. "Come on. Why don't you meet them?"

He turned and began walking.

A moment of hesitation, then McCrorie followed.

For several minutes, they pushed through the ruins of the Donovan Creek Dairy Processing Plant.

Pincombe, ever the history enthusiast, had studied up on the place. He liked knowing where he was operating. Context mattered.

The facility had belonged to Donovan Creek Creamery & Dairy, once a powerhouse of Wisconsin's dairy industry, churning out milk, butter, and cheese for the Midwest. Constructed in 1911, it had held strong through the boom years, riding on high standards and trusted partnerships with local farmers.

But by the 1960s, the industry had changed. The plant

hadn't. Bigger corporations edged out the independents. Margins thinned, losses stacked up. Then came the final nail in the coffin—a contaminated batch, a failed FDA inspection, lawsuits.

By 1969, Donovan was abandoned. Left to rot.

Now, a quarter century later, it was a husk. Sprawling twenty acres, surrounded by overgrown fields, shadowed by rusted vats and skeletal machinery. The main processing facility had collapsed in places, leaving twisted beams and shattered catwalks hanging like exposed nerves. The office building—Pincombe's current location—was still intact but barely, its brickwork cracked, staircases crumbling, remnants of long-forgotten paperwork buried under layers of dust.

The place was unstable, dangerous, and perfect for Obsidian.

This was the kind of interesting, forgotten ruin that most people never got to see. But for Pincombe, for a man in his line of work, these were the kinds of places Obsidian took him.

It had started fifteen years ago, when Pincombe was a nobody in Calgary—a small-time operator in a local Canadian crime ring, barely scraping by, running money laundering gigs and shaking down deadbeat gamblers. Nothing glamorous. Nothing important. Just another low-level hustler, another disposable name on some bigger player's ledger.

But then, a happy accident changed everything.

A rival gang leader was taken out—a car bomb that wasn't meant for him, a coincidence that left a power vacuum just as Pincombe happened to be in the right place, knowing the right people. Pincombe capitalized. Fast. Before anyone could ask too many questions, he was sitting at the big table, making decisions instead of following orders.

That's when Obsidian came calling.

They saw something in him. Ambition, adaptability, a

willingness to get his hands dirty without making a mess. They made him an offer, and Pincombe didn't hesitate. Whatever he had going in Calgary was nothing compared to what Obsidian was offering—a life with real money, real power, international reach.

For the next ten years, Pincombe bounced across seven countries in Europe, moving from one operation to the next. Arms trafficking in Serbia. A corporate sabotage job in Prague. A high-profile assassination in Madrid that still made headlines years later. He climbed fast, proving himself smarter, sharper, more efficient than the usual thug-for-hire.

Until he screwed up.

It was supposed to be a simple kill job in Berlin. Some banker who'd gotten too nosy about where his clients' money was really going. Pincombe had it handled—until he didn't. A loose end he hadn't accounted for. A civilian, a woman, saw something she shouldn't have. She ran. He hesitated. By the time he fixed the situation, the whole thing had gone sideways, too loud, too messy.

Obsidian didn't forgive mistakes.

But Pincombe had enough good will built up to avoid a bullet to the head. Instead, Obsidian exiled him—sent him to the U.S., dumped him in logistics, low-level supply chain work.

No action. No glamour. No upward mobility.

For years, he was just a bureaucratic cog—albeit a criminal cog—moving shipments, making sure the right names stayed off the paperwork, handling contracts with crooked distributors. Menial work.

But he was patient.

Pincombe rebuilt his reputation bit by bit and took every opportunity to prove himself again. It was slow, grinding, humiliating. But he did it. And now, this Plymouth cheese operation—of all things—was his chance.

A way out of obscurity.

A chance to climb back into the high life, where he belonged.

And Layne Grosicki, with his wannabe do-gooder routine, his pathetic attempt at exposing something bigger than himself, had handed Pincombe that chance on a silver platter.

Obsidian didn't just need someone to clean up the Plymouth mess. They needed someone who could run the whole damn thing.

Pincombe intended to make sure they didn't regret choosing him.

For several moments, Pincombe's mind had gotten lost in the past, in the series of events that had led to this moment of opportunity, when McCrorie's voice snapped him back to the present. They were still moving through the wreckage of the abandoned facility, stepping over rusted beams, weaving through collapsed doorways, the air thick with dust and mold.

"What about the professional? Clay?" McCrorie said. "He's getting close. He's ... figuring it all out."

Pincombe nodded. "Yes, he's caused trouble, sure. But he's not invincible. We keep the pressure on, he folds.

"Does he know about the shipment?"

"It's possible," Pincombe allowed. "But it doesn't matter. Because tonight's the night, and I'm handling the shipment personally. I have a different job for you."

He turned and strode across a stretch of perforated metal floor, patches of it rusted through entirely. McCrorie followed. They plunged even deeper into the facility's shadows, shoes clanging against more steel-grated floors, weaving their way through hallways and tangles of rusted machinery, skirting around heaps of scrap metal.

Finally, a humming sound and a light announced they'd reached their destination. They stepped into a room with a generator in the back powering a single light via an orange extension cord. In the center of the room was what had once been a dairy storage unit—a stainless steel chamber with thick bars that made it look like an oversized prison cell. Several rusted milk canisters lay tipped over inside.

Two men occupied the makeshift cell. The first was Arlo Ford, a young twenty-something Asian-American. Even disheveled from captivity, he maintained the polished look of a recent college graduate in his well-tailored business casual attire.

Beside him huddled Stuart Caruso. The *real* Caruso. A pudgy little man who also wore dress clothes, though his were far less stylish. He looked exactly like what he was: a career bureaucrat food inspector who'd stumbled into something way over his head.

Pincombe stepped forward and wrapped his knuckles against the bars. "Comfortable, gentlemen? I hope you appreciate the accommodations. This little setup is courtesy of my employers, Obsidian. They have a knack for sourcing custom accommodations around the world."

Arlo glared back defiantly while Caruso cowered in the corner.

Pincombe looked right at Arlo. "You were my insurance plan, should things get too messy with your buddy Layne Grosicki. But turns out, Layne fell right into my trap. My guys beat him to death, Arlo. *Beat* him. He begged. Cried. And in the end, we made it look like an accident."

Arlo lunged at the bars, face twisted in rage, while Caruso whimpered.

From behind, McCrorie snickered.

"I didn't need you as bait for Grosicki after all," Pincombe continued. "But this professional—Clay—is a different game. So really, thanks for being so cluelessly determined in your little quest for the truth. You stuck around long enough to be useful to me after all."

Pincombe turned to McCrorie.

"Keep an eye on them. I have some 'cheese' to ship."

McCrorie nodded.

Pincombe turned to leave. He had an appointment to make.

It was time to move some biological weaponry.

And reclaim his spot at the top.

CHAPTER FORTY

JOANNE HAD HER DAUGHTER BACK.

Sort of.

Clay had made them a team, commanding them before his abrupt departure to scour Rud's records, find a link to Arlo Ford, and then find Arlo himself.

Unlike back at the motel—when Tracy was still steaming, after all these years, still bitter—this time, she had simply taken to their urgent task, circling around the desk as soon as Clay had left and telling Joanne, "Come on!"

Practical, purposeful, and decisive.

So Tracy.

This time, there'd been no awkward moment. No lingering resentment, at least not for now.

There was no time for that, not with Arlo being held hostage somewhere unknown.

For the last ten minutes, the two women had been scouring every piece of information they could find. Sammy Rud's office was meticulously arranged, every document filed neatly, every piece of data stored in an orderly system—a reflection of the cheesemaker's methodical and disciplined nature.

Rud's organization worked in their favor, making their search easier, each labeled file leading logically to the next. Joanne and Tracy sifted through the folders, clicked through clearly structured digital records, piecing together the information.

"Here!" Tracy said suddenly. She held up a ledger, her finger tracing a series of numbers and names. "These shipments, they don't add up. There's a discrepancy here, and here..." Her voice trailed off as she immersed herself in the figures.

Joanne leaned over her shoulder...

...close enough to notice the faint crease of concentration between Tracy's brows, the way her dark blue eyes—so much like her father's, different from Joanne's bright blues—narrowed in focus.

She pushed away the swelling guilt that accompanied the thought.

Joanne shook her head, refocused, and tried to make sense of the data. "You're right. These are dummy transactions! They're meant to cover something up."

"Cover what?" Tracy said.

Joanne shook her head.

She and Tracy worked quietly, their minds piecing together the puzzle that someone had left behind in Rud's records. It was like before—years ago, when Tracy was younger, still willing to come to Joanne for advice. A twinge of nostalgia swelled within Joanne.

Then Tracy's brow furrowed.

She grabbed a notebook and jotted down every product in the suspicious transactions.

- Dairy Solids

- Organic Milk Powder
- Nutrient Additive
- Olive-Based Preservative
- Vitamin Fortification
- Acidic Coagulant
- Natural Emulsifier

She circled the first letter of each listing with her pen.

D-O-N-O-V-A-N.

Donovan.

Joanne froze. The name hit her like a gunshot.

"Clay mentioned that place!" she said. "That's where he said the shipment was happening. Where he was going to take care of business."

"I saw a map earlier," her daughter said, rummaging through the papers on the desk, throwing them to the floor until she found it. She used her palms to flatten out the wrinkled map, then traced a finger along it. "It's right ... riiiiight ... there! It's an abandoned facility on the edge of town. I saw it earlier when I was driving around, getting a lay of the land. Look." She tapped the map. "Donovan Creek Dairy Processing Plant."

A heavy silence settled between them.

Tracy's eyes flicked up to meet Joanne's, and in that instant, the same thought passed between them.

Clay had told them to stay safe.

But he'd also told them to find Arlo.

Joanne exhaled. "Clay didn't want us to go with him to Donovan."

"But he also gave us a mission," Tracy countered. "Find Arlo."

The weight of this decision sat there between them in a few moments of quiet.

Joanne's pulse pounded in her ears. Every instinct

screamed to obey Clay's original order—stay out of the fight, don't make things worse. But this wasn't just about following orders. It was about doing the right thing.

Arlo was out there. Alone.

Joanne met Tracy's gaze.

"We're going," she said.

Tracy nodded.

They rushed out of the cheese shop, going for the back entrance. As they moved, Joanne's mind was a whirlwind of emotions. The thrill of the investigation, the concern for Arlo...

...and the joy of having her daughter back.

CHAPTER FORTY-ONE

THE OUTSIDE of Donovan Creek Dairy Processing Plant was even more striking than the inside.

The moon hung high over this dead expanse of Plymouth, casting cold, blue light on the remains of the plant. Long shadows stretched over cracked concrete. Rusted machinery. Crumbling silos. The place was a specter. Silent. Forgotten. Perfect for a deal no one was meant to see.

Pincombe guided his Acura carefully through the ruins. The Donovan facility was a massive expanse of land—big enough to need a car to get from one end to the other. The prisoners he'd just left behind were stashed in the office building, but the impending exchange was to happen at the far end of the plant. Too far to walk. Too risky to waste time.

This was it. If he pulled this off—if the Plymouth operation went smoothly—Pincombe would be back on top. No more menial supply chain work. No more playing errand boy for Obsidian. This was his shot to prove himself.

One problem remained.

Clay.

That professional could blow everything apart if

Pincombe wasn't careful. But he'd planned for contingencies. Had the angles covered. He wouldn't let some outsider ruin his redemption.

In the storage space he was driving toward were two dozen steel refrigerated cases packed to the brim with artisanal cheese wheels. But this wasn't any ordinary cheese.

This cheese was laced with weaponized bacteria.

A bioweapon capable of immense damage. Worth millions. Bound for New York City. The UN Peacekeeping Gala. Target: Under-Secretary Matthias Renaud.

The implications were staggering.

The paranoid lunatics in Obsidian had insisted the exchange happen far from any populated area. They were convinced the U.S. government had eyes everywhere.

They wanted isolation. Pincombe gave them isolation. The storage building at the back of the Donovan plant was perfect. He'd scouted it months ago, made sure it met every absurd requirement.

As he approached, he spotted the Obsidian vehicles—a neat row of white panel vans.

He smirked. He could already picture the scene.

Obsidian reps in their pretentious European suits, trying and failing to blend into Middle America. A bunch of high-end sociopaths pretending to be normal.

The thought made him chuckle.

So far, everything was going exactly as planned.

His chest swelled.

Years of work. Hard damn work, clawing his way out of ruin. Risks. Betrayals. All of it led to this.

This was *his* moment to reclaim a position at the top of Obsidian's hierarchy.

But then something caught his eye.

A car. Approaching from the other side of the perimeter fence. A silver Cadillac.

For a brief second, a streetlight illuminated a face behind the wheel of an approaching vehicle—all angles and choppy strands of hair and a pair of dark eyes.

Pincombe's smirk vanished.

He knew that face.

"Clay..." he growled.

CHAPTER FORTY-TWO

Tracy's rental was a Ford Ranger. Not what she'd reserved.

At Milwaukee's General Mitchell International Airport, the rental office had claimed they were out of full-sized cars, apologized, knocked ten percent off the price, and handed her the keys to a small truck instead.

Now, after hitting potholes and curbing it twice, she was glad they had.

Something a little more off-road-ready wasn't a bad thing.

Though she doubted she was going to get her security deposit back...

Tires screaming, the Ranger plunged into the curve's apex at ridiculous speed.

Tracy heard heavy breathing coming from the passenger seat, and despite the moment's tension, she had to suppress a grin. Her mother was trying to act composed, but Tracy could see from the corner of her eye how tightly her mother was gripping her seatbelt.

Bathed in the silver glow of a blazing moon, trails of oncoming headlights streaked past. Tracy's gaze was locked in, scanning for hazards...

...and speed traps.

Mom momentarily released her grip on the seatbelt to reference the map on her lap, which they'd taken from Rud's Artisanal Cheese Shop. She squinted at it, then looked through the windshield.

She'd done a great job of navigating despite her anxiety.

And, Tracy had to admit, she appreciated her mother's focus.

"Turn left here," Mom said.

The Ranger slewed onto an older side road, suspension protesting. Tracy eased them into a sweeping turn.

Bullheaded Mom. Always steeped in her determination, never relenting until she reached her goal. This time, that stubbornness had manifested as a form of bravery. Whatever else Tracy felt toward her mother, seeing that resolve cemented trust that they would find Arlo Ford. Together.

"There!" Mom shouted over the roaring engine. "The third dirt road."

She pointed toward a rutted path appearing past a hole in the fencing. Tracy instantly spotted it and killed the headlights. She angled the Ranger onto the rough track, limbs of nearby scrub trees scraping loudly as the path swallowed them into darkness. She winced, praying the truck's paint wasn't too marred.

"Should be just over this rise," Mom said.

They crested an angled berm, chassis nearly airborne. All at once, diffuse light spilled across their path from a low structure, just visible downslope. Tracy locked the Ranger into a controlled skid. Mom smacked her hands into the dash.

And they jolted to a halt.

Ahead, bathed in moonlight, the once-imposing dairy processing plant now stood dilapidated. Its enormous steel doors and weathered brick walls were marred by graffiti and overgrown weeds. Broken windows. Strewn metal scraps. Crumbling concrete.

As soon as they were stationary, Mom bailed out and ran for the building.

More of that bullheaded bravery...

Tracy threw open her door and hurried to keep up.

Through a gaping hole in the fence.

Through a doorless entry.

And into a maze of metal and cinderblock.

"Arlo!" Mom shouted, her voice echoing. "You here? It's Joanne!"

A faint hum echoed through the still air, a distant sound that pricked their ears. Tracy's eyes lit up with recognition as she identified it.

"Generator!" she called out to Mom.

They turned down a hallway, tracking the sound, their feet crunching on the rotten concrete and clanging on steel grating. As they journeyed deeper, a soft glow began to pierce the darkness ahead of them.

They followed the light, turned a corner...

...and came face-to-face with two men behind bars.

An old dairy storage unit—stainless steel bars, heavy, solid. It looked like a prison cell. And that's exactly what it was now.

Inside, rusted milk canisters lay tipped over, forgotten. A heavy padlock and chain secured the door.

Tracy figured the young man had to be Arlo Ford. Even after captivity, exhaustion, whatever he'd been through, he still carried himself like a polished business school graduate.

But another man was with him—small and pudgy in a rumpled dress shirt and loose tie, cowering in the corner.

"Who are you?" Tracy asked the second man.

"Stuart Caruso," he replied weakly.

Tracy and Joanne exchanged a look. Tracy shook her head —questions for later. She studied the padlock and chain.

"Do either of you know where they keep the key?"

Before anyone could answer, a shadow fell across them.

Tracy spun, staring into a nightmare.

The man was of average height, average build, but imposing all the same. Broad-shouldered. Face cold and blank behind his red beard.

But it was the scars that froze Tracy. His arms, from wrist to shoulder, were a mass of twisted, puckered flesh. Burned. Mangled.

Thin red hair. Sun-damaged skin. A man who had lived hard and rough.

And his eyes—feral, unblinking.

Julian McCrorie.

McCrorie's first punch went wide, hitting nothing but air. Tracy had already moved, some more of those latent runner's reflexes coming back to life.

She saw Mom's eyes flash—first in shock, then in fury. A beat later, her mother drove a shoulder straight into McCrorie's midsection.

Damn, Mom!

They went down hard, a tangle of thrashing limbs, all technique lost to raw desperation.

Tracy darted into the fight, caught McCrorie's wrist just as his fist came hammering toward Mom's jaw. She twisted hard, feeling the grind of bone, the sharp grunt of pain.

Mom and McCrorie grappled, with the latter quickly gaining the upper hand. Tracy hung onto McCrorie's arm, dead weight, disrupting his balance, wrenching to force his arm behind his back.

But McCrorie wasn't going down easy. Wasn't slowing.

His rage only built, a wildfire spreading.

Then, with a beast-like roar, he tore free—flinging Tracy aside like she weighed nothing.

Tracy landed hard.

...on her right calf.

...where her compartment syndrome swelling had been the worst from her mad dash earlier in the day.

She screamed.

More pain as she rolled once, twice, gasping.

Vision swimming into focus, she saw Mom panting on the floor beside her—facedown, spent, beaten.

McCrorie was back on his feet. He whipped around, glowered at them.

With his eyes never leaving them, he strode to the opposite side of the room—past the cell where Arlo and Caruso watched helplessly—and to a cabinet.

He retrieved a pistol.

And walked back over.

CHAPTER FORTY-THREE

The Cadillac's V8 growled as Silence kept pressure on the accelerator, scanning the dilapidated dairy plant through the fence to his left.

Past the rusted gate blocking his path, a blue Acura closed in on a cluster of white panel vans near a storage building. He saw the driver—the man he'd known as Stuart Caruso, who was actually an Obsidian operative.

The building's door was wide open, stacks of refrigerated storage cases visible inside.

Two men in black tactical gear—high-level professionals—were already moving one of the cases into a van.

The handoff was happening.

No time for subtlety.

Silence buried the pedal. The Cadillac roared forward.

Metal screamed against metal as the sedan hit the gate. *Whack!* Sparks burst in a violent orange shower. The impact slammed Silence forward into his seat, but the Cadillac held.

Through the twisted wreckage of the gate, Silence saw the fake Caruso's eyes go wide behind the Acura's windshield. The man scrambled for the door handle.

Too late.

Silence aimed the Cadillac at the Acura's passenger side and floored it.

Whack!

Another mass impact. The second time within a few seconds.

Metal crunched. Glass exploded. Two luxury vehicles became one twisted mass. The Cadillac's excellent build quality proved itself again—two major impacts, but it was still running.

The men in the vans reacted instantly, engines gunning as the vehicles scattered. Four peeled left, while two cut right, trying to box Silence in.

But Silence was already moving.

He wrestled the wounded Cadillac through the debris field.

In his rearview, he caught a glimpse of the fake Caruso climbing woozily from his ruined Acura.

And something else caught his eye in the mirror. A red Ford Ranger parked way at the other end of the facility outside the office building.

Tracy had told him about her misadventures at the airport car rental office, ending up with a red Ranger instead of a full-size car.

Surely it wasn't *her* Ranger. He'd told Tracy and her mother to look for Arlo while he came here to Donovan.

Why the hell did they follow him here?

Unless...

Silence pushed the thought aside for the moment.

There were more immediate problems

The vans were regrouping, trying to cut off his escape routes.

He yanked the Cadillac into a hard right, tires screaming as he threaded between two pursuing vehicles. One van clipped another while trying to adjust, sending it spinning into a concrete pillar. The impact folded its side like paper.

Three down, three to go.

Silence plunged deeper into the labyrinth of the plant, the Cadillac groaning with every sharp turn and sudden brake.

Gunfire erupted.

Bullets hissed past. One caught his side mirror, tearing it off.

Silence kept his head low, weaving through the wreckage, past rusted machinery and collapsed walls.

A van appeared on his left, closing fast, trying to ram him.

Silence waited.

One beat.

Two.

Then he hit the brakes.

The van shot past, too late to course-correct. It plowed straight into a fallen steel beam.

The impact sent it cartwheeling, end over end.

And when it came to a stop, smashing into a concrete wall, it exploded.

Two left.

They were smarter now. Keeping distance. Trying to wear him down.

And it was working.

The Cadillac was dying. The engine knocking, frame groaning with every turn. Wasn't going to last much longer.

Silence spotted a gap between two silos and took it, metal screaming, sparks illuminating the dash as the Cadillac scraped through.

One van followed.

The other circled ahead, waiting.

Perfect.

He'd led them exactly where he wanted—into a narrow corridor of wreckage.

The van behind him closed in. The one ahead lurched into position, blocking his exit.

Silence waited.

A breath. A second.

Then he yanked the wheel hard.

The Cadillac slid sideways. The pursuing van had no time to stop.

It smashed into its partner in a violent collision, metal on metal, thunderous and final.

But that was it for the Cadillac.

The engine coughed, sputtered, died. Steam hissed from under the hood.

Silence had loved the car...

Dammit.

He pulled himself out through the shattered window, boots hitting the ground just as he caught movement ahead.

Two figures emerged from the wreckage of the last van. One carried an AR-15— not exactly welcome, but nothing Silence hadn't handled before.

Then moonlight glinted off something mounted beneath the rifle's barrel, something that changed the equation entirely.

An M203 grenade launcher.

CHAPTER FORTY-FOUR

Joanne's heart pounded as she stared down the barrel of McCrorie's gun, the steel glinting in the dim light. Beside her, Tracy was struggling to rise, her face tight with determination.

The odds weren't in their favor.

A sudden blur of movement and a clang of metal.

McCrorie jerked, eyes going wide, then collapsed in a heap.

Joanne blinked. Looked down. A rusted metal rod clattered on the floor, rolling to a stop under McCrorie's limp hand.

She turned, following the path from which the rod had come.

Arlo was still behind the bars, arm extended through the gap, a lopsided grin on his face.

He'd thrown it.

He gave her a shrug. "Figured I should contribute."

Painfully, Joanne got to her feet and carefully pulled the gun from McCrorie's loose fingers and slid it across the floor.

She unhooked the keyring from his belt loop with the same caution, then hurried with Tracy to the metal cage.

As Joanne used the key to unlock the padlock, a shout from Arlo made them spin around: "Look out!"

McCrorie was back on his feet, blood streaming down his face, his eyes wild and unfocused. He lurched toward them with outstretched hands, looking absolutely deranged.

They moved as one, Tracy leading the charge, Joanne, Arlo, and Caruso flanking in sync.

McCrorie swung wildly at Tracy, but she saw it coming, ducked cleanly, fluidly, without hesitation. Before he could recover, she countered fast, grabbing his arm and twisting hard.

Joanne felt a surge of pride. Her daughter wasn't just reacting—she was controlling the fight.

As McCrorie turned to lunge again, Caruso slammed a shoulder into his back, forcing him off balance. The big man staggered. Joanne moved to sweep his legs, but Tracy was already there, hooking her foot behind his knee, toppling him.

McCrorie hit the floor hard. Arlo lunged in, locking down one arm. Tracy took the other.

"Move!" Tracy snapped, already forcing McCrorie toward the cage. She didn't need instruction.

Joanne followed, watching as Tracy and Arlo muscled him forward, his thrashing no match for their momentum. With a final, brutal heave, they shoved him inside.

Joanne slammed the door and threw the bolt, but it was Tracy's steady hands that locked the padlock.

Through the bars, McCrorie glared at them, chest heaving, looking like a caged animal. He was trapped now, just like he'd trapped the others.

Pulling her cellular phone from her pocket, Tracy checked the multiplex. "I'll call Clay."

Joanne nodded. "Honey?"

Tracy looked up, finger on her phone's buttons.

"Proud of you," Joanne said.

Tracy stared back at her for a moment. Then smiled.

CHAPTER FORTY-FIVE

PINCOMBE SLAPPED a hand against the Acura's mangled fender, stopping himself from toppling over.

His head swam. His whole body ached. He blinked fast, trying to clear the haze, vision swimming through the shattered remains of his windshield.

Clay had come out of nowhere.

First, ramming through the gate in a blaze of sparks.

Then ramming *Pincombe*. At full speed.

Before climbing out of the wreck, Pincombe had tried to reverse. Slammed the gear shift. Stomped the gas. The Acura had made a horrible screech. Didn't budge. Fully incapacitated.

That asshole Clay had wrecked him good.

Movement.

Pincombe turned.

Out ahead, the last two Obsidian operatives were advancing, rifles up, fanning through the wreckage, closing in on Clay's previous position.

Pincombe grinned.

One of the men had an M203 grenade launcher strapped under the barrel of his AR-15.

That would solve the Clay problem.

The professional had caused too much trouble, a constant thorn in Pincombe's side. But even Clay wasn't dodging an explosive round. Any second now, the night would light up, and that would be the end of it.

But...

Pincombe's fingers drummed against the steering wheel.

If Clay survived.

Somehow.

Some way.

If Clay killed the rest of the Obsidian contingent, then Pincombe needed a backup plan.

His exit strategy had just shifted. His car was dead. His men were dead, all but two. His business here was finished.

But that didn't mean he was out of options.

Not yet.

Wincing, he shoved into the door. It creaked, stuck. He tried again, harder. Pain lanced through his ribs, but the door gave, and he stumbled out onto the pavement.

His body screamed at him. He gritted his teeth. Kept moving. There was no time for pain. He'd been through worse than this.

He wobbled toward the storage building. The one with the shipment.

Since the Acura was totaled, there was no way to get an entire metal case out of here. Too heavy to carry or even drag.

But he could still take a piece.

He yanked the door open, coughed as dust swirled inside, then threw open one of the metal cases.

Inside—wheels of cheese.

Perfectly aged. Perfectly dangerous.

Pincombe grabbed one, stuffed it under his arm like a football.

Then he started walking.

The processing plant's grounds were massive, stretching across acres. And now he had no car, no backup, no easy way out. He was going to have to walk all the way back to the office building.

His legs felt like lead. The crash had left him reeling, but he kept moving.

One unsteady step at a time.

And the whole time, he felt ridiculous.

Clutching a single wheel of cheese.

But this cheese could save his life.

If Clay destroyed the rest of the shipment, Obsidian would be furious. They'd hunt him down. But if he delivered even one wheel, he had leverage.

One wheel was all it took. Obsidian could reverse-engineer the bacteria.

The weaponized strain had been developed in secret labs beneath Chicago, months in the making. A bioweapon disguised as something so trivial, so ordinary.

Obsidian might still want him dead after so much was botched here in Plymouth. True.

But they'd hesitate first.

If he had the cheese.

Pincombe staggered forward, the cheese wheel tucked under his arm like a sacred relic.

Maybe this wouldn't get him back into the high life.

But it would keep him breathing.

Still, just in case, there was another backup plan.

The prisoners.

Clay had a soft heart. Pincombe had seen that immediately. It wasn't something you could fake—not when a man carried it like a weight.

That was Clay's weakness.

And if the cheese wasn't enough, the prisoners would be.

One way or another.

But none of that mattered if Clay didn't make it past the final two Obsidian operatives.

And their grenade launcher.

Pincombe paused, staring into the darkness where Clay had disappeared, the two Obsidian men on his trail.

He waited.

Listened.

Any moment now, the night would light up, tear apart.

Any moment now...

CHAPTER FORTY-SIX

SILENCE DARTED behind the rusted shell of a massive, broken-down machine as the first explosion tore through the night.

The force shook the skeletal remains of the plant. Silence shielded his eyes as a fireball of steel and concrete ripped through the wreckage just feet behind him.

That grenade launcher was a problem.

A major problem.

Dust and grit stung his eyes. His heart slammed against his ribs. Two targets left—the last of Obsidian's team.

One had a Glock.

The other had a damn grenade launcher.

And they were hunting him.

Silence peeked around the edge of the ruined machine, saw the two black-clad operators advancing through the debris. They moved with skill, coordinated angles, no wasted motion. Not the usual hired muscle.

High-end professionals.

The Glock guy flanked left while the grenadier held back,

ready to drop another round at the first glimpse of movement.

Silence gritted his teeth.

They were boxing him in.

Another breathy thump.

Silence didn't hesitate. He dove.

And the world split open.

The machine exploded behind him, flipping like a toy, flaming metal shards slicing through the air. Silence hit the ground, rolled hard. Heat seared the back of his neck.

C.C.'s voice came, urgent. *Move, love! Move!*

Silence scrambled to his feet, bolted off.

The Obsidian operatives were herding him, pushing him deeper into the remains where a large, black void awaited.

No cover. No exits.

They wanted to end this quick.

Not happening.

Silence stayed low and fast, using the smoke and wreckage to mask his retreat. He slipped behind a crumbling concrete barrier, forced his breath steady. He needed a plan.

Glock guy first.

Then, he would deal with the grenade launcher.

He adjusted his grip on the Beretta, flexed his fingers once, then moved.

A shadow flickered through the smoke ahead—Glock guy, closing in fast.

Silence exploded forward.

Gun up. Two shots.

The first clipped Glock guy's forearm. The second punched through his thigh.

The man staggered, grunted in pain, tried to raise his weapon—

Too slow.

Silence was already there.

He crashed into the man's injured leg, dropped him hard. The man shrieked.

A gunshot screamed past Silence's ear, instant tinnitus—a wild shot, off target.

Silence caught Glock guy's wrist, twisted. The weapon clattered to the pavement.

One clean, brutal strike to the throat, and the man crumpled.

"No—" the man started to shout.

Too late.

Crack! Crack!

Silence shot him twice in the face. A double tap. His preferred method. He wiped blood off his knuckles.

One down.

No time to breathe.

Because now it was just him and the grenadier—and the grenadier still had all the firepower.

Footsteps. Not far away.

Silence gritted his teeth. The grenadier was moving now, slow, deliberate. Reloading.

Another thump.

Silence bolted.

And the world went white.

An explosion erupted to his side, throwing him forward, ears ringing from the blast.

He hit the ground hard.

Dust. Heat. The taste of copper in his mouth.

Silence rolled, pushed himself up, feet unsteady.

Another grenade whistled through the air.

He sprinted.

Another blast.

This one ripped through his path, flames licking at his heels as he dodged behind a half-collapsed structure.

The grenadier was toying with him now. Pinning him.

Keeping him off balance.

Silence crouched behind the cracked wall, mind racing. He needed to shift the fight, change the dynamic. Sweat dripped down his cheeks. He licked blood from his lips.

He peeked out— and froze.

Through a busted window, past the wreckage and smoke, he saw movement on the far side of the facility.

It was the man he knew as Stuart Caruso.

The bastard was still alive.

Wobbling. But moving, making his way across the grounds.

And he was clutching something under his arm—a wheel of cheese.

Silence's eyes narrowed.

That wasn't just cheese. That was the weaponized product.

And the man was heading straight for the office building.

...where Joanne and Tracy had gone.

Silence's gut tightened.

The office building—that must be where the other prisoners were. *That* was why the red Ranger was parked outside.

Another thump.

Another blast.

Silence yanked back as the explosion tore through the side of the building, debris raining down. The structure groaned, weakening.

One more hit, and the whole damn thing would collapse.

His eyes snapped to the grenadier.

The man was reloading, calm, confident.

Too confident.

Silence moved. Fast. He cut through the falling debris, kicking off a crumbling ledge, landing low. Gun up.

The grenadier registered the movement, spun—

Too late.

Silence fired.

One. Two. Three. Center mass.

The grenadier staggered back, arms windmilling, whacked into a wall...

...but remained standing.

Body armor.

Silence closed the distance. He grabbed the grenade launcher's barrel, yanked down, twisted. The man fought back, shoving forward.

They slammed into a half-toppled support beam, struggling, twisting for control. Silence tore the rifle away.

The man snarled, shifted his weight, tried to break free.

And Silence released him.

He allowed the man to take off, go running through the rubble.

When he was several yards away...

...Silence fired.

The explosion was instant.

The men went airborne, sucked backward into a fireball.

His smoking remains crumpled into the wreckage.

Silence shielded his eyes, panting, as debris settled around him. He stole one final breath, eyes snapping to the office building—where the Obsidian leader, the man he'd been calling Caruso, had just disappeared.

Silence gathered his strength and took off at a dead sprint.

CHAPTER FORTY-SEVEN

Pincombe's chest heaved, boots scraping over the debris-strewn floor. Sweat dripped from his face despite the cool night air, and the Glock 19 in his grip felt heavier than usual. He cursed the weight of it. Cursed the situation.

Cursed the name Clay—the relentless ghost that had dismantled everything Pincombe had built.

He could still hear the faint sounds of pursuit—Clay closing in. Muted footfalls. Steady. Measured. Like the man had all the time in the world. But Pincombe knew better.

That wasn't patience.

That was precision.

Clay was hunting him. Pincombe had been hunted by professionals before. But never any this good.

His only advantage now was the building itself.

He'd only been in town for a few days but studied this facility from afar, from Brooklyn, for months. Knew every rusted pipe, every sagging beam, every blind corner. Even in darkness, the layout was imprinted in his mind. Clay may have been the predator, but Pincombe had the upper hand here.

He reached the lobby area.

Enormous stainless-steel beams glowed blue in the dim light, illuminated from above by shattered skylights. Pincombe's boots crunched broken tile. He darted between the pillars, taking sharp turns to mask his trail—just in case Clay was right behind him.

Then he stopped. Pressed his back against cool metal. Listened.

Nothing.

His breath slowed, lungs burning, the sweat on his skin turning cold. He wiped his brow, adjusted his grip on the Glock.

Yes, Clay had been a ghost up until now. Picking apart his operation without a word.

Here, though, Pincombe could turn the tables.

He had the home-field advantage.

"I know you're out there, Clay," he called, voice echoing through the cavernous space.

He stepped out from behind the pillar, moving toward the executive office wing.

"By the way, we've never been formally introduced." He let out a short, dry laugh. "The name's Alan Pincombe. And guess what? You're in my home now. I know every inch of this rotten place."

He listened. Nothing.

Pincombe gritted his teeth. No response. He hadn't expected one. The man was too disciplined.

Fine.

If Clay wanted to play the ghost, Pincombe would draw him out another way.

"You've been a real nuisance to me, Clay," he said. "But I'm about to cross you off my list of headaches."

Still nothing.

Pincombe's grin faltered.

Clay wasn't rattled by taunts. The man was methodical. Unnervingly so.

Pincombe moved toward the executive offices. The glass walls were cracked, fogged yellow-green with grime. He ducked into one of the rooms, brushing past a splintered doorframe.

The room was cluttered with old desks, file cabinets, papers strewn across the floor. He crouched behind a desk, peering through the jagged remnants of a glass partition.

And there he was.

Clay.

Emerging from the lobby, moving with eerie calm. His silhouette was sharp against the dim light.

He was only yards away.

And he hadn't spotted Pincombe.

Pincombe fought back a snicker as he watched the man pause, tilt his head ever so slightly.

Listening to the building itself.

Pincombe raised the Glock. Steadied his aim. He exhaled, lined up the shot.

His finger tightened on the trigger—

And Clay darted to the side.

Fast.

One second, he was there. The next, gone. Before Pincombe's finger even finished squeezing the trigger.

Crack!

The round punched a hole in the wall beyond, sheetrock exploding.

Okay, he was wrong. Clay *had* known where Pincombe was.

Pincombe dropped down, heart hammering. He hadn't expected Clay to be that fast. Or perceptive.

He took off, ran to the other side of the room, slid behind another desk.

The plant fell into quiet again. Nothing but the slow drip of water from a leaking pipe.

Pincombe tightened his grip on the Glock, scanning the room, heart thundering.

He needed to stay ahead. Keep Clay guessing.

He slipped out of the room, moving into a narrow hallway that led to a storage area. It was darker here, the shadows deeper.

...but Pincombe could still feel Clay closing in.

Then, however, his familiarity with the building paid off.

He took a set of spiral stairs and reached the rickety overhead walkway. Stopped. Glanced at the precariously balanced stack of old metal beams.

He grinned and shifted his weight onto the walkway.

It groaned. Loud.

The sound echoed through the plant, which would alert Clay.

Sure enough, the footsteps behind Pincombe quickened.

Clay's shadow appeared below. Approaching fast.

Pincombe ducked into an alcove, reached out, and shoved the stack of beams.

They teetered...

...wobbled...

...then crashed down in a thunderous clatter.

A grunt. A sharp thud.

Had he done it? Was Clay dead?

Pincombe stepped out of the alcove and peered over the walkway's edge.

Clay was down.

Pinned under one of the beams, shoulder visibly strained. Blood smeared his temple, glinting in the dim light.

For the first time that night, Pincombe allowed himself a genuine smile.

He stood up.

And began descending the stairs.

CHAPTER FORTY-EIGHT

THE BLOOD WAS WARM. Sticky. Making a dark patch on Silence's shirt that grew larger with each breath. Not good. But not fatal either.

Sure hurt like hell, though.

Silence lay motionless under the twisted heap of metal debris, listening to the steady *tap-tap-tap* of expensive shoes on marble. Italian leather. Maybe Ferragamo, if Silence had to guess.

"You're bleeding, aren't ya, Clay?" Pincombe's voice floated down from above. Smug. Satisfied. "You're hurt. I can hear it in your breath. Can't hide that."

Silence didn't move. Didn't respond. Just counted the footsteps. Getting closer. Nine feet away. Maybe eight. His ribs screamed with each breath, but that was secondary. Irrelevant. What mattered was the moment. C.C. had taught him that.

Be aware of what is, she'd said. *Not what if.*

"Been studying this place for months." Pincombe's voice echoed off the walls. Not shouting. Not whispering. A conversational tone. Like they were having coffee. "Been on the ground here a week. Know every inch. Every corner. Every shadow. You were just stumbling around my own personal playground."

Silence ignored the searing pain in his ribs, focusing instead on Pincombe's position. The man's boots scraped over the debris-littered floor, the sound faint but growing closer.

"That's the thing about knowing the lay of the land." Closer now. Six feet. "You can turn it into a damn trap."

Silence almost laughed at that last statement, the near-irony of it.

Because the debris he was lying so theatrically beneath had merely grazed him when it fell.

It hadn't crushed him.

But Pincombe didn't need to know that. Not yet.

Silence waited until Pincombe was almost upon him...

...then, in one explosive motion, Silence burst upward, metal clattering away.

"But... but..." Pincombe stammered, eyes wide with shock. "You were—"

One brutal punch to the gut cut off his words.

Pincombe gagged as he doubled over. Silence caught his wrist and twisted hard, sending the Glock clattering across the floor.

He followed with another hit—a savage elbow that connected squarely with Pincombe's jaw.

Teeth snapped, and blood spattered across the concrete as Pincombe collapsed, coughing and spitting red onto the floor.

Silence stood over him.

The man's hands came up, pleading.

"Wait. *Wait!*" Pincombe coughed, gasping. "We can... talk. We—"

Silence didn't hesitate.

Crack! Crack!

Two shots to the head. Silence's beloved double tap.

Pincombe's body jerked once, then stilled.

Silence stared at him for a moment, observing the nothingness, the death.

Then, across the room, something rolled against the floor, bumping against the far wall and tipping over, coming to a stop.

The wheel of cheese.

Silence walked over, crouched down.

Where Pincombe had struggled to manhandle the thing, stuffing it under his arm, Silence palmed it easily.

The weight of it meant something now. He would get this to the Watchers. They would find the deadly material inside, decipher it.

Obsidian's operations in Plymouth were handled.

But Silence wasn't done in the old Donovan Dairy office building.

Arlo. The real Stuart Caruso. The women.

And Julian McCrorie, unaccounted for...

Silence took off at a run.

CHAPTER FORTY-NINE

TRACY FELT ALMOST as trapped as the man she'd locked in the barred room behind her.

Because the weight of the past half hour was getting pretty damn heavy.

Arlo, who had come through for them with an act of unexpected heroism, had apparently expended his reserves of youthful vitality. Now he was slumped in the far corner, back against the wall, eyes half-lidded, blinking slow and heavy. His arms hung limp over his knees.

Across from him, Stuart Caruso didn't look much better. He shifted uncomfortably on a broken chair. The small man looked entirely out of his depth, the kind of guy who never expected to be involved in something like this. His tie was loose, his shirt rumpled, but he was still trying to keep himself composed.

Next to Tracy, Mom provided a strong and steady presence. She'd taken it upon herself to rally everyone's spirits.

Tracy exhaled. "Are you sure Clay will know what to do?"

Mom nodded. "Yeah, Clay will know. I haven't known him much longer than you, but... yeah, he'll know what to do."

She said it with a smile and utmost certainty. She'd put a lot of faith in Clay over a very short period.

Tracy started to answer—

Then movement.

A flicker to her right. Too fast. Too quiet.

She gasped, whirled, heart slamming against her ribs...

It was Clay.

Standing in the doorway.

For a beat, Tracy couldn't breathe.

How the hell did he get in without a sound? It should've been impossible for a massive guy like him. But he moved like mist.

Her mother turned, relief flashing in her eyes.

Caruso blinked rapidly, looking unsure of what to do. Then, after a beat, he spoke, his voice timid. "Um, hi. You must be Clay. I'm Stuart Caruso."

Clay's eyes flicked to him. A nod. Nothing more.

He scanned the room, took everything in. His eyes stopped on McCrorie, locked up in the makeshift holding cell.

Clay said nothing, just moved.

Tracy and Joanne stepped aside.

Clay strode toward the back area, the makeshift jail cell, his presence filling the room.

Inside, beyond the bars, McCrorie was waiting, standing in the center of the space, his face twisted into a sneer.

Clay stopped.

Their eyes met.

"You worked..." Clay said, swallowed. "For Obsidian?"

"Yeah."

"You kill..." Swallow. "Layne Grosicki?"

"No."

"Others?"

"Damn right. I killed plenty others. What of it?"

"All I needed..." Clay said, swallowed. "To hear."

Crack! Crack!

Deafening noise. *Literally* deafening.

Tracy screamed, hands flying to her ears as the world went deaf, lost in the ringing.

Clay had moved in a blur, pistol out before Tracy even registered it.

Two shots.

Both through the bars.

Both into McCrorie's head.

Blood and tissue exploded backward and splattered the wall. The body slumped to the floor.

Mom was stunned, shaking.

So was Arlo. So was Caruso.

Tracy didn't move, didn't speak.

Clay turned to her, which made her jump and take a half-step back.

As the ringing in her ears subsided slightly, she heard Clay tell her, "Take care of them." He motioned to the others. Swallowed. "Get back to hotel." Swallow. "Meet you there later."

He stepped between Tracy and her mother, heading for the doorway.

"Where are you going?" Tracy called.

Clay met her gaze. "To find Harvey."

CHAPTER FIFTY

The Ford Ranger's tires screamed as Silence brought it to a sliding halt outside the garage.

He'd borrowed the truck. Tracy's rental. His Cadillac was now deceased.

Watchers Specialists had finally cracked it—Harvey's coordinates. Phone traces, cell tower pings, and digital breadcrumbs had led to this location, a squat garage on Plymouth's outskirts. Not much to look at. Rust on the walls.

And spray-painted hollow skull designs everywhere.

Silence remembered what the Specialist had said.

Their symbol—that hollow skull—shows up as graffiti where they're active. It's a warning sign.

And...

Their signature move is skull-crushing. Literal skull-crushing. Bats, sledgehammers. Bodies turn up in Lake Michigan, faces unrecognizable. It's their calling card.

Silence's hands curled into fists.

He heard something from inside: the sound of fists striking flesh. Then, a muffled grunt.

His fists squeezed tighter.

He circled the perimeter and peered through one of the gaps to the stark, dusty interior. He counted the enemies. Seven total. Six muscle, one boss. All carrying. From what he could see, a mixture of pistols and SMGs, the cheap kinds. Amateur hour.

Harvey and the young man from the pawnshop—Jesse, Silence now knew his name to be—sat dead center tied to metal folding chairs. Both bleeding. Harvey's shirt was torn to hell. Jesse's face was swollen and pink. But they were alive. That's what mattered.

The big man had to be Mateo Vargas. "El Gordo." Three hundred pounds of prison muscle in a wife-beater. Tattoos like poison ivy up his arms. He was talking. Harvey was listening. For once in his life, Harvey was actually listening.

Silence found his entry point—a personnel door with rusted hinges. The lock was child's play, more straightforward than the lock at Rud's Artisanal Cheese Shop had been. He waited for the patrol pattern to cycle, then slipped inside.

The garage's interior was a maze of tool benches and partially dismantled vehicles. The air reeked of oil and something metallic but not mechanical—blood. Silence moved between cover points, closing the distance. One of the gangsters passed within arm's reach, completely oblivious.

"Your friend better show." Vargas's voice carried. A boss's voice. Used to being obeyed. "Or we start removing pieces."

"He'll come," Harvey said. His voice was uncharacteristically powerful despite the split lip. "He always comes."

Silence allowed himself a fraction of a smile.

Then, it was time to make an entrance.

He stepped into the light. "Looking for me?"

Every head in the place snapped toward him. Weapons raised. Metallic clicks. Vargas's face split in a predatory grin.

"You must be the man with the money."

"I have money," Silence said, swallowed. "But you're not getting it."

The nearest thug's finger tightened on his trigger.

But Silence was already moving.

His first shot took the man in the throat before he could squeeze off a round. The second caught his partner in the chest as he brought his SMG to bear.

Chaos erupted.

Silence rolled behind an engine block as bullets chewed the concrete where he'd just been standing. He came up shooting, two more precise shots dropping a gunman who'd been trying to flank.

The man's SMG clattered across the floor.

"Kill him!" Vargas roared.

Silence moved through shadows. Appearing. Disappearing. Each shot perfect. Each movement planned. The garage worked for him now. Tight angles. Bad sight lines. But he made it work.

Besides, the opponents were far from hardened warriors. Yes, amateur hour indeed. All bravado, no substance.

Automatic fire pushed Silence behind a tool chest, lead pounding through the sheet metal.

Pop! Pop! Pop!

He counted rounds. Waited for the click. There it was. Empty magazine. By the time he heard it, he was already moving. His elbow caught the shooter's throat. A knee strike folded him.

The man hadn't hit the floor before Silence engaged his next target.

Knee. Solar plexus. Another one on the concrete.

Four down.

The last two got sloppy, desperate. Spray-and-pray, spitting out wild shots that sparked off metal and concrete.

Silence dropped one of them with a double tap through a car window.

The other tried to run. Silence's shot caught him in the back of the head.

Six down.

Only Vargas remained.

The gang leader had Harvey in front of him now—untied and upright—with a massive arm locked around Harvey's throat. His pistol was pressed against Harvey's temple.

Classic move. Predictable.

"One inch closer," Vargas snarled, "and his brains paint the wall."

Silence stood perfectly still, Beretta aimed.

Forty feet. Bad angle. And Harvey was in the way. There was a lot of mass behind the target—a lot of Vargas—but Silence didn't have the shot.

Harvey made eye contact.

Silence's trigger finger moved a millimeter.

"You really think—" Vargas started.

Crack!

Silence's round went through the eye.

He'd had a better shot than he thought.

Harvey stumbled forward as Vargas's body crashed like a redwood behind him. For a moment, the garage was silent save for the ringing echo of the gunshot.

Silence moved quickly, grabbing a knife from one of the workbenches to cut Jesse free and to cut the ropes remaining on Harvey's wrists and ankles. Harvey trembled.

Jesse staggered to his feet, pale and shaking. "Thank you," he stammered. "I... I should... I should...."

Silence nodded. "You should go."

Jesse didn't need to be told twice. He vanished into the shadows, footsteps receding until there was the squeak of hinges, leaving Silence alone with Harvey and seven cooling bodies.

Harvey was staring at Vargas's corpse. "I just wanted to help Jesse. He was in trouble with these guys over some loans. I thought... I thought I could talk to them." He looked up at Silence. "I'm not very good at talking, am I?"

Despite everything—the firefight, the rescue, the dead men steaming on the concrete—Silence laughed.

He rarely laughed out loud.

But he did now. At the absurdity he'd just heard.

"You talk plenty," he said and swallowed. "Let's roll."

He turned to leave. Harvey followed.

CHAPTER FIFTY-ONE

The next morning

JOANNE'S EYES BLINKED OPEN, squinting.

Morning sunlight poured in through the hotel suite's sheer curtains. She'd forgotten to shut the thicker outer drapes before she fell asleep.

For a moment, she lay disoriented, blinking against the brightness, wondering why she was in a hotel room.

Then she remembered. All of it.

She was in Plymouth, Wisconsin.

Ah, yes.

Everything came back, including the events of the previous night, which hit her like a flood—the tension, the revelations, the sudden, brutal violence of Clay's extrajudicial execution. With all that behind her, she'd been too drained to think or even feel much when she'd stumbled into the suite with Tracy.

She glanced down at the sofa she was sprawled on. She hadn't even unfolded the sleeper couch portion, just collapsed onto the cushions and slipped into a deep, dreamless sleep.

As Joanne sat up, her back protested the awkward position she'd slept in. She groaned. Stretched.

Her eyes went to the closed door of the bedroom. She'd insisted Tracy take the bed.

Tracy.

Her daughter.

Asleep in the next room.

Tracy had been through hell and back last night. They both had. Watching her daughter navigate the chaos of the previous twenty-four hours was like looking at a younger version of herself—determined, resourceful, and far too willing to carry burdens.

As if summoned by her thoughts, Joanne heard the bedroom door click open.

Tracy stepped out—sweatpants, oversized sweatshirt, chestnut brown hair slightly mussed.

"Morning," Tracy said. Her voice was soft, full of morning grogginess. She padded into the central area of the suite.

"Morning."

"You sleep okay?" Tracy motioned toward the sofa.

Joanne gave a slight shrug. "Can't say it was the best sleep I've ever had. You?"

Tracy shrugged. "Meh."

Her daughter moved toward the kitchenette, and Joanne noticed the limp.

It was subtle but noticeable.

Joanne remembered what Tracy had told her last night in those few fleeting moments of open conversation before exhaustion took them both.

Tracy suffered from compartment syndrome. A bicycle accident. Seattle. Years ago.

Joanne hadn't known.

Watching her daughter limp, she wondered what else she

didn't know. How many other injuries? How many struggles? How much had Tracy carried alone?

The thought settled deep in Joanne's chest, landing heavy and painful.

Tracy reached the counter and set about boiling water, pulling two mugs from the cabinet. "Tea okay?" she asked over her shoulder.

"Perfect."

Joanne leaned back against the couch cushions and watched as Tracy made the tea.

When Tracy brought the mugs over, she handed one to Joanne and sat across from her in an armchair. They sipped together in quiet contemplation.

"Tracy," Joanne said finally. "Can we... can we try again? To have a relationship?"

Tracy didn't hesitate.

"No," she said.

Joanne blinked. There hadn't been anger in her daughter's voice. Nor cruelty. It was just finality.

For a moment, Joanne started to protest—to explain, to justify, to plead. But she stopped herself.

Her eyes drifted to the journal resting on the end table beside the sofa. The pages were filled with moments of self-reflection, admissions she wouldn't have been capable of even days ago.

She read the words branded on the cover:

YOUR PAST
IS NOT YOUR FUTURE

That could be interpreted in multiple ways, she now realized. Good and bad.

Plymouth had changed Joanne.

Clay had changed her.

But changing now didn't undo what she had been before. It didn't erase the years of being a monster to her daughter. To so many others.

She let out a slow breath.

She would accept what she was given.

Tracy shifted, setting her mug down. "We can't have a relationship yet," she said.

Joanne swallowed hard, nodding, accepting.

Then Tracy exhaled, glanced away for a beat, then back.

"But... maybe someday." A pause. Then, softer, "How about we start with the occasional phone call?"

Joanne felt an immense weight lift.

"That would be wonderful," she said.

CHAPTER FIFTY-TWO

South Beloit, Illinois

The rest area sprawled beneath towering oaks, an island of concrete and picnic tables dropped into the wilderness.

Silence sat on a sun-warmed concrete table, his Johnston & Murphy brogues planted on the bench below, watching the shadows of leaves dance across the pavement. Highway traffic hummed in the distance, a steady rhythm.

That sound pulled at something deep inside Silence. He'd always loved this part of the job—the endless highways, the hours on the road. Time alone. Mile after mile after mile of... well, silence. Both with a capital and lowercase S.

Rest areas like this were a particular comfort. Something about their static nature, their controlled tranquility. Green lawns. Foot trails. Yawning, stretching travelers.

This one was just across the state line—an Illinois state welcome center. The main building was a pleasant-looking brick affair with a glass front entrance surrounded by a wooded area with picnic shelters, a cluster of vending machines, and a dog walk. Tidy shrubbery. Fragrant mulch. Charming. Well maintained.

Among interstate rest areas, the state welcome centers were far and away the nicest. States liked to make a good first impression on visitors.

After the "detour" in Wisconsin, Silence had a long road trip ahead of him to California. One that would normally be great, a fantastic opportunity to decompress.

Normally.

But this trip had a companion. Harvey. Who was in the bathroom, probably reorganizing the paper towel dispensers.

Silence's phone buzzed. The multiplex display showed Doc Hazel's number. He exhaled, delayed, considered evaporating from existence, then flipped the phone open.

"Ma'am?"

"Well done, Suppressor," Doc Hazel's clinical tone crackled through the line. "Specialists have already taken action with the work you accomplished in Wisconsin. Initial analysis indicates Obsidian's biological weapons program has been effectively dismantled. Their plan to embed weaponized bacteria in artisanal cheese shipments has been neutralized. The UN Peacekeeping Gala and Matthias Renaud are no longer at risk."

Silence grunted acknowledgment.

"I've received your three letters," she continued, her transition characteristically abrupt. "A successful completion of our alternative therapy."

Silence waited...

"The first letter was fine," Doc Hazel said, "expressing your resentment toward the fellow Asset. Years of pent-up anger over his betrayal in Boston. Therapeutic, wouldn't you say?"

Silence didn't respond.

"The second letter was better, addressing the civilian

injury in Missouri. The guilt you've carried over that accident. Important to confront these buried emotions, Suppressor. Good. Very good."

Silence didn't respond.

A crow landed nearby and pecked at discarded french fries, avoiding the ketchup remnants.

"But it's the third letter that interests me most," Doc Hazel continued. "Written to Harvey King. Examining how your previous mission together two years ago affected Harvey's life in ways you hadn't acknowledged. The impact of your dismissal of his contributions, your refusal to see the humanity beneath his... quirks."

Silence shifted on the table.

"Okay, Suppressor, what did this exercise teach you about human connection? Tell me how you feel."

Feelings. She always wanted to discuss his damn feelings.

Silence's throat was particularly raw after the activities of the last several days. He gave it a preemptive swallow. "That sometimes..." he said and swallowed again. "We affect others more..." Another swallow. "Than we know."

A long pause filled the line. For a moment, Silence thought the connection had cut out. He checked his phone.

When Doc Hazel spoke again, her tone had softened fractionally. "Stunning. Simply stunning. You've made some real progress, Suppressor."

Silence didn't respond.

"Now... have fun on your road trip with Harvey."

Beep.

The line went dead.

She just couldn't leave without being a smartass. Just couldn't do it.

Silence stared at the phone for a moment before pocketing it. The crow was still struggling with the French fries, which were mashed into the pavement.

He heard a door open and turned around. Harvey emerged from the men's room, stepped over to the drinking fountain, wetted his fingers, and flicked a few droplets on Mitsy. He then dropped the air plant into his left breast pocket and hurried toward Silence.

"Clay, did you know that the historical development of rest area plumbing systems actually follows a fascinating progression of regulatory guidelines?"

Silence shook his head.

"The paper towel dispensers in there were completely misaligned with optimal user traffic flow patterns. I took the liberty of implementing a new arrangement based on ergonomic principles that—"

"Time to go," Silence said, already walking to his new car, a Watchers-provided BMW that had replaced his poor, deceased Cadillac. The Bimmer was a 3 series, coupe, black, brand new. He'd parked it in the shade of a cherry tree, and shadow-filtered sunlight glistened off the car's polished surfaces.

Silence slid behind the wheel and started the engine, which came to life with a delightful purr. Harvey climbed in, pulling a receipt from his pocket to fold.

Silence backed the car out, and a few moments later, they were on Interstate 90 again heading south. The highway stretched ahead, endless and empty. Somewhere to Silence's right, to the west, waaaaay out there in California, a safe house waited for Harvey, the man's new life.

Between here and there lay hundreds of miles of highway.

This would normally be a comforting notion for Silence—the long drive, all that time to think and exist. To be free.

But this time, there was Harvey to his side.

Silence looked at him. The guy was unusually quiet, particularly engrossed in the folding of this specific receipt, for some reason.

Maybe it wasn't such a bad thing to have Harvey there in the passenger seat during this upcoming road trip. There was something endearing about Harvey's earnestness, his complete lack of pretense.

Silence's missions involved facades and deception—constant chess moves with dangerous players. Harvey, though... Harvey was exactly who he appeared to be.

In that way, he reminded Silence of C.C.

Maybe having someone genuine along for the ride wouldn't be the worst thing.

Especially if he remained quiet like this.

Silence set the cruise control, relaxed back into his seat. The steering wheel's leather wrap was brand new—smooth and clean and perfect under his fingers. The new-car smell was strong. The climate control, perfect.

Yes, another road trip was ahead of Silence. Open highway. Mental freedom.

He caught himself almost smiling.

"Oh!" Harvey exclaimed, breaking the quiet so suddenly that Silence jumped in his seat. "Did you know that the concrete mixing ratios used in interstate highway construction have actually evolved through several distinct phases since 1956? The fascinating thing about aggregate composition is..."

The half smile remained on Silence's face.

But he had to fight to keep it there.

FREE SILENCE JONES BOOK

If you enjoyed reading this Silence Jones thriller, I kindly ask that you leave a review on Amazon. It only takes a minute, but it makes a huge difference.

How about a free Silence Jones thriller?

As a thank-you for being a reader, I'd like to offer you *DEADLY SILENCE,* a novella you won't find on Amazon. It's exclusively available as an ebook to members of the Erik Carter Readers Group. To grab your copy, just sign up at www.erikcarterbooks.com.

MORE SILENCE JONES MISSIONS

The Silence Jones missions continue with Book 15, ***STEALTH TACTICS,*** available for pre-order soon.

Stay tuned for further updates at www.erikcarterbook s.com.

ALSO BY ERIK CARTER

Ty Draker Action Thrillers

Novels:

Burn It Down

Raw Deal

Novella:

Point-Blank

Silence Jones Action Thrillers

Novels:

The Suppressor

Hush Hush

Tight-Lipped

Before the Storm

Dead Air

Speechless

Quiet as the Grave

Don't Speak

A Strangled Cry

Muted

In the Dead of Night

Tell No Tales

Unspoken

Dying Breath - coming soon

Novella:

Deadly Silence

Dale Conley Action Thrillers

Novels:

Stone Groove

Dream On

The Lowdown

Get Real

Talkin' Jive

Be Still

Jump Back

The Skinny

No Fake

Novella:

Get Down

ABOUT THE AUTHOR

ERIK CARTER is the author of multiple bestselling action thriller series.

To find out more, visit www.erikcarterbooks.com.

ACKNOWLEDGMENTS

For their involvement with *Dying Breath*, I would like to give a sincere thank you to:

My ARC readers, for providing reviews and catching typos. Thanks!

Printed in Great Britain
by Amazon

58604559R00159